# A Final Shoot-Out

When Abe Fletcher is released from prison, he is anxious to reclaim his inheritance – a particularly beautiful and flourishing ranch. At the same time, bank robbers Red Ned Davis and Hank Jolley, are fleeing from justice and holed up with Jolley's cousin, Vic Morgan.

After a chance encounter between Abe and Vic, the outlaws agree to help Abe regain his inheritance – for a price.

However, their plans go awry due to the unexpected intervention of a seductive saloon singer, Arizona Audrey, and the famous Kentuckian gunfighter, Jack Stone. And, when the chips are down, there is nobody deadlier than Stone.

# A Final Shoot-Out

J.D. Kincaid

**A Black Horse Western**

ROBERT HALE · LONDON

© J.D. Kincaid 2015
First published in Great Britain 2015


ISBN 978-0-7198-1632-1

Robert Hale Limited
Clerkenwell House
Clerkenwell Green
London EC1R 0HT

www.halebooks.com

The right of J.D. Kincaid to be identified as
author of this work has been asserted by him
in accordance with the Copyright, Designs and
Patents Act 1988
Typeset by
Derek Doyle & Associates, Shaw Heath
Printed and bound in Great Britain by
CPI Antony Rowe, Chippenham and Eastbourne

# AUTHOR'S NOTE

In this novel I am re-introducing the reader to an old acquaintance of Jack Stone, namely the seductive saloon singer, Arizona Audrey, who previously featured in *Sharkey's Raiders*.

JCD

# SEPTEMBER 1879

# CHAPTER ONE

It was Saturday night and the hands of the Triple F ranch, the biggest spread in Bridger County, were heading towards the small Wyoming cow-town of Snake Springs, so named because at its inception it was over-run by rattlers, copperheads and various other serpents. Since then the town had grown and now was home to approximately three hundred people, the snakes in the meantime having been pretty much eliminated.

At the head of this cavalcade of cowboys were Abe and Brett Fletcher, the two sons of Robert B. Fletcher, owner of the Triple F. Immediately behind the brothers rode Lew Todd, the ranch foreman, and behind him, riding two abreast, were six of the Triple F's hands. As for Robert B. Fletcher, he rarely rode into town on a Saturday night, preferring to remain at home on the ranch with his beloved wife, Emily.

Of the two brothers, Abe the elder was the one who had inherited his father's looks, while Brett took after his mother.

Abe was a tall, handsome young man, blond with a pair of piercing blue eyes and strong clean-cut features. He possessed an air of total confidence, almost arrogance, and was not slow to exploit his position as heir to Bridger County's largest and most successful ranch. Unlike the foreman and six cowhands who accompanied him and Brett into town, he had done more than simply change his working shirt for a fresh one. He had donned his best Stetson, black and low-crowned, a fine white linen shirt, black bootlace tie, Prince Albert coat and Sunday best trousers and boots. All in all, he cut a fine figure on his splendid chestnut stallion.

Brett, on the other hand, had followed the example set by the hands and had simply replaced his sweat-soiled check shirt with a clean one. He continued to wear his everyday grey Stetson, brown leather vest and denim pants. Anyone who did not know him would have taken him for one of his cowboys. But then, unlike his brother, Brett was quiet and self-effacing. Although not small, he was nowhere near as powerfully-built as Abe and presented a much less imposing figure. Also, his pleasant, boyish features and calm grey eyes served to complement his mild, easy-going manner.

However, despite their totally different characters, the two brothers were close. Both enjoyed their work on the ranch and were trusted and respected by Lew Todd and the other hands. But, whereas Abe had a hot temper and could at times be unnecessarily high-handed, Brett invariably remained even-tempered. In consequence, the cowboys preferred, when and where possible, to work with the younger brother.

The church clock struck seven as the nine horsemen came to a halt in front of Snake Springs' only saloon, the Lucky Chance. They quickly dismounted, hitched their horses to the rail outside, and then clattered up the flight of wooden steps and on to the stoop. At their head, Abe Fletcher pushed open the batwing doors and the others followed him into the saloon.

The saloon was like a hundred or so others in cowtowns across the West. It consisted of a large bar-room, with stairs at one end leading to the bedchambers upstairs, where the saloon's sporting women entertained their customers. Downstairs was a long mahogany counter behind which the bartenders, Sid and Barney, dispensed beer and whiskey to Snake Springs' thirsty citizens. There were also a roulette table and several other tables and chairs, where a mixture of townsfolk, cowboys and homesteaders sat happily drinking and chatting or playing the two games of chance on offer: blackjack and poker. The remainder of the Lucky Chance's customers stood three-deep at the bar. Overhead, lighted kerosene lamps hung from the rafters and at either end of the bar-counter stood a spittoon. All in all, the bar-room presented a lively, rumbustious and colourful scene.

Abe Fletcher shouldered his way through the crowd to the bar and promptly ordered nine beers. This was a weekly tradition. Then, after the first round of drinks, the Triple F cowboys would be expected to buy their own.

Abe's first beer went down in one swift, continuous draught and straightway he ordered a second. This caused Brett and the foreman, Lew Todd, to exchange worried glances. Abe was inclined to gulp back his drink in double-quick time when in a bad mood. They knew this from past experience. And both had feared the worst before they set out. He had, they surmised, been bottling up his anger since the event that had caused it.

It was like this: that afternoon, Abe and Brett had been in the corral breaking in mustangs. Both were superb horsemen and expert wranglers, but there is no wrangler alive who has not, from time to time, been thrown when breaking in a wild horse. And that was Abe's fate earlier that day. Unfortunately, Abe regarded the mishap as a humiliation. His fierce pride was severely dented and now he was proposing to drown the memory of the event in drink.

Brett recalled the few previous occasions when his elder brother had ridden into town in a foul temper. Each time, Abe had ended up in a brawl of his own making. On all but one occasion, Brett and the others had succeeded in dragging him away and back to the ranch before the law intervened. On that one occasion, however, Marshal Jeff Huston had arrested

Abe and thrown him into a cell at the rear of the law office. On the following morning, Robert B. Fletcher had paid the fine needed to release his son and, since then, there had been no further such incidents. Brett prayed fervently that another would not take place that evening. He liked and admired his brother, but could not understand the other's feeling of mortification. Brett certainly did not enjoy being thrown, yet, like most other wranglers, he accepted that this was bound to happen sometimes. And, when it did, he simply re-mounted the mustang and got on with the job. He did not feel in any way humiliated.

Both Brett and the grizzled and experienced Triple F foreman determined to keep a close eye on Abe and, as discreetly as possible, encourage him to slow down his beer consumption. But this was no easy task. Surrounded by his hard-drinking hands, Abe was in no mood to moderate his intake. He continued to throw back beer after beer as fast as he was able.

And so the evening progressed. Saturday nights at the Lucky Chance were invariably lively affairs and this one proved to be no exception. Sid and Barney were given no respite: there was much raucous laughter and the saloon's sporting women were kept in constant demand, forever disappearing upstairs with a succession of lustful clients.

Keeping a watchful eye on the proceedings were the saloonkeeper, Joe Dunn, and his trouble-shooter,

Vince Preston. Dunn, immaculate as always in his grey three-piece suit and Derby hat, and Preston, huge and menacing and dressed all in black from his Stetson to his boots, had both observed that Abe Fletcher was not in the sunniest of moods. They had been quick to recognize the signs, for it had been in the Lucky Chance that Abe had previously lost his temper and ended up picking fights.

'I think I'd best warn the mayor that there could be trouble here tonight,' Dunn whispered to his trouble-shooter after spying on the young rancher for a couple of hours and judging that he might shortly erupt.

'Should I ask Abe to leave?' growled Preston.

The saloonkeeper frowned and shook his head.

'No, Vince,' he said. 'We don't wanna provoke him. Mebbe he'll jest settle down an' it'll be OK,' he added, though without much conviction.

Then, leaving Preston to continue his vigil, Joe Dunn made his way across the bar-room to the table where the mayor and various other of the town's dignitaries were sitting, drinking and conversing together. Earlier that evening, they had been in the mayor's office to plan Snake Springs' annual Autumn Fair and now, with their plans laid, they were intent upon relaxing and enjoying the rest of the evening.

As Dunn approached the table, a tiny, spindly, shabbily-dressed, grey-haired figure almost collided with him.

'Watch where you're goin', Willie,' said Dunn, as he stepped adroitly aside.

'Oh . . . er . . . sorry, Mr Dunn.'

Willie Malone grinned nervously. He was clutching several empty glasses and was on his way to the bar with them. Slow-witted, but ever willing and amiable, Malone had spent most of his sixty-odd years doing all manner of odd jobs in and around the town. At the present moment, he was employed by Joe Dunn to collect up empty glasses and wash them ready for future use. He continued on his way while the saloonkeeper addressed the mayor, Frank Lawford.

Lawford was flanked on his right by his deputy, the town's one and only lawyer, Lionel Smith, and on his left by the local physician, Doc Griggs. All three were soberly dressed in similar attire: city-style suits and Derby hats. But here the resemblance ended, for the mayor was small, round-faced and jolly-looking, his deputy tall, rake-thin and of a hawkish visage, while the doctor was large, stout, red-faced and bespectacled. They and the others at the table broke off their conversation in order to hear what Joe Dunn had to say.

'I don't wanna alarm you, Mr Mayor,' said Dunn quietly. 'But I don't reckon Abe Fletcher over there is in the best of tempers, an' you know what that means.'

'Indeed we do,' replied Frank Lawford. 'Lionel, the doc an' I were all present on that night Abe got hisself arrested.'

'What are you proposin' to do, Joe?' enquired Lionel Smith.

'I dunno. Watch him I s'pose, an' try to stamp out any trouble 'fore it starts.'

'Hmm. Mebbe we should drink up an' go, fellers? It's gittin' late anyways,' said the mayor.

'That might be best,' concurred Doc Griggs.

The others seated at the table murmured their agreement. They had no wish to get caught up in any brawl. However, at that moment Abe Fletcher suddenly announced in a loud voice that he fancied tumbling one of Joe Dunn's sporting women. Although the hubbub in the bar-room was sufficient to prevent them from hearing his exact words, they soon divined his intentions, for, almost immediately, he barged through the drinkers lining the bar and, with a petite young brunette on his arm, proceeded upstairs.

Lawford smiled up at the saloonkeeper.

'I reckon we could risk another round of drinks after all,' he announced.

'Hear! Hear!' exclaimed his companions.

'Same again, gents?' asked Dunn and, on obtaining their assent, he said, 'I'll go fetch 'em.'

On arriving at the bar, he gave the necessary order to the bartenders and, while he waited for them to pour the drinks, got into conversation with Brett Fletcher and Lew Todd.

'Your brother didn't look too happy this evenin',

he remarked to Brett.

'Nope.'

'Somethin' upset him?'

'He was breakin' in a hoss an' got thrown,' said Lew Todd.

'That's right. It's happened to us all, but Abe always takes it real bad,' sighed Brett.

'Wa'al, mebbe a tumble upstairs with Belle will bring a smile to his face?' said Dunn.

'I sure hope so,' declared Brett. 'I don't want Marshal Huston havin' to arrest him again. Last time, Pa was madder'n a grizzly in a bear-trap an' Ma – she was so upset!'

'I don't figure it'll come to that, boss,' said Todd, crossing his fingers behind his back.

'No, 'course not. Belle'll settle him down,' reiterated Dunn, hopefully. Then, as Sid and Barney placed the two trays full of drinks on the counter, he called across to Willie Malone, who was busily washing the glasses he had just retrieved. 'Hey, Willie! Gimme a hand with one of these trays!'

'Sure thing, Mr Dunn,' replied the odd-job man.

The pair conveyed the two trays across the bar-room to the mayor's table. Then, having handed out the drinks to Frank Lawford and his fellow dignitaries, they picked up the empty trays. Dunn handed his to Willie Malone.

'Take 'em back to the bar, Willie,' he ordered. Then, turning to the mayor, he said, 'Sorry if I worried you unnecessarily.'

17

'Don't give it a thought. All's well that ends. . . .'

But Lawford never finished his sentence, for at that instant a series of piercing screams rent the air. Immediately, the bar-room hubbub ceased and all eyes peered upwards towards the railed balcony on the upper floor. Behind it lay a narrow corridor, on either side of which stood the Lucky Chance's bed-chambers. It was from one of these that the screams were emanating.

Willie Malone was passing the foot of the stairs when the first scream was heard. Immediately, the old man plonked down the two empty trays on to a nearby table and hustled up the stairs towards the upper floor. Slow-witted he might be, but Malone had earlier seen Abe Fletcher leave the bar-room with the sporting woman on his arm and consequently deduced that it was the young brunette who was screaming.

And so it proved. As Willie Malone reached the upstairs balcony, a crimson-faced Abe Fletcher erupted from one of the bedrooms. He was hastily pulling on his clothes as he proceeded along the corridor towards the balcony and Malone saw that his knuckles were covered in blood.

'What in tarnation have you been doin'?' demanded the little odd-job man.

'None of your goddam business!' rasped Abe.

There was a heart-rending wail behind him and Belle staggered out into the corridor, stark naked and with her body showing a multitude of bruises

18

and her face splattered with blood.

'Goddammit, you've gone an' beaten Belle up!' exclaimed Malone. 'Why would you do that?'

' 'Cause he couldn't git it up!' cried Belle.

'Whaddya mean?'

'He'd had too much to drink an' couldn't perform. Which made him mad an' so he took it out on me!' she replied tearfully.

'Shuddup!' Abe rounded on the girl and yelled, 'You want me to beat you up some more, you li'l whore?'

'No, you don't!' cried Malone, and the little old man scuttled along the corridor and bravely threw himself at the brawny young rancher.

But he was no match for Abe. Two vicious punches to the jaw sent him reeling backwards along the corridor, across the balcony and crashing into the balustrade. The rancher followed him and, as the old man slumped back against the rails half-conscious, Abe stooped down and grabbed him round the legs.

'This'll teach you to meddle with me!' snarled Abe and he straightway heaved Willie Malone up and over the balustrade.

Gasps from the crowd beneath and a cry of 'Oh, my God, no!' from Belle were succeeded by a dull thud and then a short period of silence.

Moments later, Vince Preston, who had followed Willie Malone up the stairs, grabbed Abe from the rear and twisted one arm up behind his back in a half-Nelson. Abe tried to twist free, but failed. He

19

swore and attempted to strike Preston with his other fist. To no avail. Preston grabbed the youngster's flailing arm and twisted it, too, up behind his back. Then he frog-marched Abe downstairs. On their way down, the pair passed a couple of Joe Dunn's sporting women running upstairs to tend to the battered and bloodied Belle.

When Vince Preston and Abe Fletcher reached the bar-room, they found that the crowd below had gathered in a circle round the fallen body of Willie Malone. Kneeling beside the odd-job man and examining him was Doc Griggs and at the physician's left shoulder stood the mayor, Frank Lawford.

'Wa'al, Doc, what's the verdict?' demanded Lawford *sotto voce*.

Doc Griggs shook his head sadly.

'There's nuthin' I can do. I'm afraid Willie's dead,' he declared.

'Jeez! I'd best send for the marshal,' growled Joe Dunn.

He was saved the trouble, however, for one of his customers had already left the saloon and sprinted across to the law office to inform the marshal of what had just happened.

In consequence, as Joe spoke, Marshal Jeff Huston pushed open the batwing doors and entered the saloon.

Huston was a tall bean-pole of a man, grey-eyed, thin-faced and sporting a drooping black moustache. He was in similar attire to Abe Fletcher, though, instead of a black Stetson, he wore a black Derby hat and his badge of office was pinned to the front of his coat. In his late forties, Huston had kept the law in Snake Springs for almost twenty years. He was a dour, taciturn fellow, yet a dedicated peace officer, both admired and trusted by the citizenry.

'OK, folks – tell me what happened!' he rasped, upon reaching the spot where Willie Malone lay dead.

'Willie fell from the balcony,' said the mayor.

'I can see that. But how did he come to fall? There's a balustrade up there an' it don't look broke to me,' stated Huston.

'It ain't,' growled Vince Preston. 'Abe Fletcher heaved him over.'

Huston turned to face the young rancher, who remained held fast by Joe Dunn's trouble-shooter.

'Whaddya gotta say to that, Abe?' he demanded.

'It . . . it was an accident. I . . . I didn't mean to . . .' spluttered Abe, ashen-faced. The shock of having been responsible for Willie Malone's death had all of a sudden both sobered and frightened him. 'We . . . we was jest brawlin' an' Willie fell back agin' the rails an' somehow toppled over,' he said quietly.

'That's a lie!'

Huston glanced upward towards the balcony. Belle stood there, flanked by her two colleagues. One had wrapped a gown round the girl and the other had wiped some of the blood from her face.

'What are you sayin', Belle?' asked the marshal.

'I'm sayin' that Abe deliberately lifted an' threw poor Willie over that thar balustrade,' said Belle.

'No, that ain't true!' cried Abe.

'Yes, it is!' rasped Vince Preston. 'I was steppin' on to the balcony when Abe tipped Willie over, an' I saw it all as clear as day. Belle's tellin' the truth, Marshal. That weren't no accident.'

'OK. So, what started all this trouble?' enquired Huston.

'Let me explain,' said Joe Dunn. 'Abe had mebbe had a few too many beers when he took Belle upstairs. I . . . I figure it didn't go quite accordin' to plan up there an' Abe lost his temper an'. . . .'

'Blamed me!' cried Belle. 'Then he started beatin' me an' when I screamed, Willie came runnin' to my aid.'

'Yeah. Yeah, that's all true. But . . . but I didn't mean to kill the ole feller. I punched him a coupla times, that's all. He jest lost his balance an' fell backwards over the balcony. I swear it!' protested Abe, desperately trying to convince himself of his innocence, though in his heart of hearts he knew that, fuelled by alcohol and a foul temper, he had acted exactly as Belle and Vince Preston claimed.

'You're lyin',' said Vince Preston firmly. 'You was in one helluva temper when you got here, an' were lookin' for trouble.'

'Is that so?' said Huston.

'I s'pose,' confessed Abe reluctantly.

'He was thrown by a hoss he was breakin' in earlier

22

today. Not somethin' that happens to him very often. I guess it hurt his pride,' interjected Lew Todd.

'That's right,' confirmed Brett. 'Abe's a darned good horseman an' was upset that he'd been thrown. But, even so, I can't believe that he intended to throw Willie down from that balcony.'

'There are two witnesses say he did,' said Huston. 'What, if anythin', did you folks down below see?'

'Not a lot,' confessed Joe Dunn.

'Willie fell back agin' the balustrade an' then, the next thing we knew, he was fallin'. I sure as Hell couldn't say whether or not Abe intentionally heaved him over,' remarked Frank Lawford.

'Nor me,' said Lionel Smith.

'Nor me,' added Doc Griggs.

'Nobody else got anythin' to add?' asked Huston.

There followed some murmuring, but nobody spoke out.

'So, whaddya plan doin', Marshal?' demanded the mayor.

'I ain't got no choice.' Huston turned to face Abe Fletcher. 'I'm arrestin' you for the murder of Willie Malone,' he said.

'No! No, you can't! I ain't no murderer!'

Despite the young man's protests, Huston clapped a set of handcuffs on his wrists and marched him out of the saloon and across the street to the law office. He was followed by Brett Fletcher, also protesting, and the rest of the Triple F outfit. If Brett had any idea of trying to spring his brother, the sight of two

23

of Huston's deputies stepping out on to the sidewalk, brandishing shotguns, quickly dispelled it.

'Go fetch Pa! He'll soon git me outta here!' yelled Abe, as he was dragged into the law office.

'OK, Abe. We'll be as quick as we can,' promised Brett.

Thereupon, he and the others returned to the front of the saloon and swiftly untied their horses and mounted them. Moments later, Brett, Lew Todd and the six Triple F cowhands galloped off down Main Street, heading back towards their ranch. Behind them, a crowd had gathered on the Lucky Chance's stoop to watch them go, while inside the saloon the mayor and a few others remained grouped round the corpse of Willie Malone.

'What now, Frank?' asked Doc Griggs, rising from where he had been crouching beside the dead body.

'I guess we go git Jasper Bartlby to take poor ole Willie over to his funeral parlour,' replied Lawford.

'Yup. Then I suggest we head back to the bar, for I sure could use a drink,' declared Lionel Smith fervently.

'Hear! Hear!' said the mayor.

In the event, they downed several more that night and were still drinking and discussing the matter of Willie Malone's death when Brett and his companions eventually reached the Triple F and rode up to the ranch-house.

As they pulled up their horses, Lew Todd growled, 'Guess you an' the boss'll be headin' back to town to confront the marshal. D'you want me an' the boys to ride with you?'

Brett shook his head.

'Nope,' he said. 'I figure if Pa can't persuade Marshal Huston to release Abe, nobody can. You boys bein' there ain't gonna make no difference, but thanks for the offer.'

While the others went off to stable their horses, Brett dismounted and clattered up the short flight of wooden steps to the ranch-house. He found his father and mother in the large dining-cum-living room that occupied most of the house's floor-space. Although the fire was unlit, they were sitting on either side of the fireplace, reading. Robert Fletcher was flicking through the *Bridger County News* while his wife Emily read *Persuasion*, a novel by her favourite author, Jane Austen. Both looked up in surprise as Brett burst into the room.

'You're back early,' commented Robert.

'Yeah.'

'Where's Abe? Isn't he with you?' enquired Emily.

Brett hesitated and stared down at the floor.

'Wa'al, answer your mother,' barked Robert.

'No. No, Abe ain't here,' mumbled Brett unhappily.

Emily paled. She was a small, petite, very pretty woman in her mid-forties. She and the two boys' father made a handsome couple. A graceful, gentle creature, her face remained youthful and unlined and her hair only lightly touched with grey. Now her bright blue eyes showed a hint of anxiety.

He husband had also picked up on his son's discomfiture, and he recalled only too clearly the last time Abe had failed to return from Snake Springs with the others.

'Out with it, Brett. Tell us what's happened,' he ordered.

'Abe's been arrested,' replied Brett glumly.

'What for? Has he gotten himself involved in some brawl?'

'Yessir.'

'Wa'al, he can jest cool his heels there till mornin'.'

'Aw, Robert, can't you go bail him out?' enquired Emily anxiously.

'No. He's gotta learn to control that hot temper of his, Emily,' stated the rancher.

'But. . . .'

'Pa won't be bailin' him out either now or in the mornin', Ma,' said Brett.

Robert turned to stare at his younger son.

'Whaddya mean?' he demanded.

'Abe ain't comin' home. There's gotta be a trial first.'

'A trial? What in tarnation is he gonna be tried for?'

'Murder, Pa.'

'Murder!' cried Robert and Emily Fletcher simultaneously.

'Yeah. He . . . he killed li'l Willie Malone. Threw

him off the balcony in the Lucky Chance saloon.'

'Oh, my God!'

While her husband exclaimed, Emily burst into tears and buried her head in her hands. It took some moments before father and son could console the grieving mother sufficiently for her to cease weeping.

'You'd better explain,' ordered Robert.

'It was like this, Pa,' began Brett, and he went on to describe the events that had taken place that evening in the saloon.

When he had finished, there followed a period of quiet while his parents digested what he had told them. It was his mother who spoke first.

'I can't believe that Abe would have deliberately killed that old man,' she sobbed. 'It must've been an accident.'

' 'Course it was,' said her husband. 'Wasn't it, Brett?'

'Wa'al, I'm sure Abe didn't initially set out to kill him,' said Brett, yet he could not bring himself to deny that, in the heat of the moment, Abe had indeed purposely heaved Willie Malone up and over the balustrade.

'Come on, we'll go an' confront the marshal,' said Robert. 'I'm sure I can persuade him to release Abe,' he assured his wife.

But he was wrong. When he and Brett confronted Marshal Jeff Huston in the Snake Springs law office, he found that the peace officer would not be moved. Huston informed the rancher that he had two witnesses who would swear Abe had acted deliberately, with malice aforethought.

'An' that, in my book, amounts to murder,' Huston stated adamantly.

'But. . . .'

'There are no buts, Mr Fletcher. Your son will stay in jail until I can arrange for his trial to be held.'

'But will he git a fair one? The folks round here were kinda fond of ol' Willie an'. . . .'

'Abe's trial will be held in the county seat, an' I'm sure you'll have no complaints regardin' the fair-mindedness of the Jamesville jury,' said Huston.

'I see.'

Robert Fletcher stared grimly at the marshal. As the wealthiest rancher in Bridger County, he knew he could have persuaded most of the county's town marshals to release Abe on bail. But Jeff Huston was not a man who could be either bullied or bought. The rancher sighed resignedly. Abe would have to remain behind bars until his trial in Jamesville, when Robert prayed that the jury would find him not guilty.

# CHAPTER TWO

Two weeks later, Elmer Atkins, the circuit judge, arrived in Jamesville and put up at the Moose Head Hotel. He was scheduled to try Abe Fletcher for the murder of Willie Malone the next day. And, since Judge Atkins had a reputation for handing out severe sentences, it was considered certain that, should Abe be found guilty, he would hang.

The judge was a spare, conservatively-dressed fifty-year-old, black-suited and given to wearing a black stovepipe hat. He had a rather pale complexion, austere features and was both harsh-visaged and gimlet-eyed. Upon descending from the noon-day stagecoach, Atkins summoned a porter to fetch his portmanteau and then entered the hotel. He had been assigned the hotel's best chamber, upstairs overlooking Main Street, and, weary after his long coach-ride, he ordered luncheon to be brought to his room. He intended firstly satisfying his appetite and then, secondly, taking an afternoon nap.

29

Shortly after Judge Atkins' arrival in Jamesville, Robert Fletcher, his wife Emily and son Brett rode into town. They left their carriage at the Moose Head's livery stables and entered the hotel. Their rooms were, like the judge's, upstairs, but, unlike him, they chose to take luncheon in the hotel dining-room. Not that any of them had much appetite. Indeed, Emily ate scarcely anything at all, so worried was she about the possible outcome of the forthcoming trial.

At the conclusion of their meal, Emily turned to her husband and said nervously, 'Robert, when Marshal Huston informed us of the date of the trial, he also told us the name of the presiding judge.'

'That's right, my dear: Judge Elmer Atkins,' replied the rancher.

'An old acquaintance of yours, you said.'

'Yes. We fought together on the Union side during the Civil War.'

'So, you are friends?'

'Were friends, Emily. We haven't been in contact in years. Not since hostilities ceased and the Confederates surrendered.'

'Still, couldn't you have a word with him?'

'To what end? It's the jury who'll decide Abe's fate, not Elmer.'

'But it's he who'll pass judgment should Abe be found guilty. He'll decide upon the appropriate sentence.'

'I guess.'

'So, perhaps you could ask him to be lenient?'

'That would hardly be proper.'

'Our son's life is at stake here!'

'I realize that, Emily. But, if I am seen approachin' the judge . . .'

'Then, make sure you are not seen, Robert.'

'I don't even know where he's stayin', my dear.'

'Mebbe I could find out, Pa?' suggested Brett.

Robert Fletcher turned to his son.

'An' jest how d'you propose to do that?' he asked.

'There's a saloon across the street. I could go buy me a coupla beers an' keep my ears open. I reckon the trial is sure to be the talk of the town. An' there's every chance someone will mention where the judge is residin'.'

Robert stroked his jaw thoughtfully.

'Hmm. You could be right,' he muttered.

'It's at least worth a try, Robert,' urged Emily.

'Yeah, I guess so.' The rancher eyed his son closely and said, 'But don't go askin' no questions, Brett. I don't know whether I can persuade Elmer to take a lenient view, but he sure as Hell won't if'n' he thinks his integrity is likely to be compromised.'

'Don't worry, Pa. I'll be as discreet as I can,' promised Brett.

'OK. We're goin' up to our room. If you do find out where Elmer's holed out, come an' let me know,' said Robert.

'Sure thing, Pa.'

Thereupon, they rose and left the dining-room,

the rancher and his wife heading upstairs, while Brett stepped outside the hotel and proceeded across the street towards the saloon.

It was almost two hours later when he tapped lightly on the door of his parents' bedchamber. It was opened immediately by his father and he swiftly stepped inside.

'Wa'al?' enquired the elder Fletcher anxiously. 'Did you find out?'

'Yeah, Pa, I sure did,' Brett grinned. 'He's jest along the corridor. Two doors down, in fact.'

'How'd you know that? Did you ask someone?' demanded Robert B. 'You know I said not to,' he rasped.

'I didn't need to, Pa,' retorted Brett. 'Folks was talkin' 'bout the trial like we reckoned they would, an' one of 'em pointed at an upstairs window in this here hotel. He said that was the exact room in which Judge Atkins is stayin'. So, all I had to do was count the windows to figure out where his room was in relation to ours.'

'Well done!'

'Oh, yes! Thank you, Brett!' cried Emily. Then, turning to her husband, she said, 'OK, Robert, now it's up to you.'

'Yes, my dear,' he replied and, accompanied by Brett, promptly left the room.

Judge Elmer Atkins was awake and looking out of the window at the busy scene unfolding in Jamestown's Main Street, when Robert Fletcher tapped on his door.

'Come in!' he barked. His expression changed to one of consternation, as the rancher entered and hastily closed the door behind him. 'Robert? What in tarnation are you doin' here?' he exclaimed.

'I needed to see you, Elmer,' stated Robert.

'But that's most improper when I'm soon to be presidin' over the trial of your son for murder!'

'That's why I'm here.'

'Now, look here. . . .'

'We were comrades-in-arms once.'

'I know, Robert, but. . . .'

'During the Battle of Gaines' Mill I saved your life.'

'I guessed you were gonna mention that.' Atkins' features were grim. His eyes blazed angrily. 'Did anyone notice you enter this room?' he asked.

'No.'

'But someone's sure to have seen you enter the hotel.'

'I'm stayin' here, as are my wife an' younger son.'

'Oh, God!'

'So, we are all residin' at the Moose Head. So what? It's the best hotel in town. Where else would we stay?'

'Even so!'

'Nobody can know for sure that we've met.'

'When they find out we're at the same hotel, folks are bound to speculate.'

'Let 'em.'

'That's easy for you to say, Robert. It's my reputation that's likely to be at stake.'

'I know an' I wouldn't ask you this, but I'm desperate. You owe me your life an' I'm afraid I'm callin' in that debt.'

Atkins sighed.

'What do you want of me?' he asked.

'I think you can guess,' said Robert.

'Yeah, but still, you'd better spell it out.'

'OK. Should my son Abe be found guilty of murderin' Willie Malone, I want you to give him a custodial sentence.'

'You figure he will be found guilty?'

'I don't know. But, if he is, I jest don't wanna see him hanged. If that was to happen, it'd kill my wife, I know it would.'

Elmer Atkins nodded. He could understand his old comrade's dilemma. Robert Fletcher probably felt bad about taking advantage of the fact that the judge owed him his life, yet he clearly believed he had no choice in the matter. He must, at all costs, save his elder son's life. While Atkins appreciated that, he still resented having his integrity compromised in this way.

'If the worst happens, I'll see what I can do,' he promised morosely.

'You won't impose the death penalty?'

'I've already said, I'll see what I can do,' muttered Atkins through clenched teeth.

The rancher wanted a rather more definite

34

pledge, yet was reluctant to press the judge further. He feared, should he do so, he might alienate Atkins completely and do more harm than good.

'OK,' he said. 'Thank you.'

'Goodbye, Robert.'

The judge's dismissal was final. There was nothing more to be said other than 'farewell'. And, so, Robert Fletcher took his leave of him.

Neither man slept well that night. Both were looking somewhat strained when the trial commenced at 10 a.m. on the following morning.

Robert B. and his younger son sat at the rear of the courtroom, where they could see everything without themselves being observed by all and sundry. Emily remained in her room at the hotel. Her husband had no wish that she should be subjected to a detailed description of the awful events that had taken place at the Lucky Chance saloon. As far as he was concerned, the less she knew the better. To that end, he had arranged for her sister to arrive in town that morning from nearby Crowfoot City, and sit with her until the trial reached its conclusion.

The opposing counsel were alike as chalk and cheese, since Robert B. had hired Samuel Brevington, a hot-shot lawyer from Chicago, to defend his son, while the public prosecutor was a local man and native of Jamesville, Dan Elam.

The former was tall and elegant and inclined to berate the witnesses. The latter, on the other hand, short and fat, and slow and deliberate of speech, treated them rather more gently. He had none of Brevington's arrogance and flamboyance.

Witnesses for the defence were as follows: Brett Fletcher; Lew Todd and two of the Triple F cowboys; Joe Dunn; the mayor and his deputy; Doc Griggs and four more of Snake Springs' citizens, who had attended the Lucky Chance on that fateful night. But, although Samuel Brevington did his darnedest to persuade them to state categorically that Abe Fletcher had not heaved Willie Malone over the balustrade, that the old man had accidently toppled over it, he failed signally to do so. All any of them would admit was that he could not be sure one way or the other. Even Brett and the others from the Triple F felt unable to swear on oath that it was accidental, though all four stated emphatically that they could not believe Abe had meant to kill the old man. However, in each case, Dan Elam forced them to admit that, from where they stood in the bar-room below, it was impossible to see exactly what had happened on the balcony.

As for the witnesses for the prosecution, the hot-shot lawyer had even less success with them.

Firstly, he tried to break down the young sporting woman.

'Miss Belle Busby?' he enquired, with a smile, once she had been called forth.

'Yes,' she acknowledged nervously.

'On the night in question you were plying your trade as usual at the Lucky Chance saloon. Is that correct?'

'Yessir.'

'An' how would you describe your occupation?'

'I'm a sportin' woman.'

'A prostitute, in other words?'

'Er . . . I s'pose so.'

Belle eyed the counsel coldly. She preferred the term 'sporting woman', but sensed that it would be unwise to say as much.

'Not a profession any decent woman would embrace,' pronounced Brevington, his voice loaded with contempt.

Belle said nothing.

'Have you no view on the matter?' he enquired derisively.

'No.'

At this juncture, Judge Atkins intervened.

'Pray stick to the matter at hand, Mr Brevington,' he snapped. 'It is what the witness saw that the jury is interested in, not what she thinks.'

'Very good, your Honour.' The lawyer looked less than happy at the judge's intervention, but dared not challenge him. Instead, he did as instructed and turned to the witness and said, 'Please describe the events, as they occurred that evening, from the time you and the accused went upstairs.'

'Yessir.' Belle gathered her thoughts and then proceeded, slowly yet succinctly, to describe how Abe Fletcher, upon finding himself incapable of performing in bed, had lost his temper and started beating and punching her. 'My screams brought Willie runnin' upstairs. An' when Abe an' I stumbled out into the corridor an' Abe threatened to beat me some more, Willie tried to stop him,' she stated. Thereupon, she paused as she pictured the scene, her mind in turmoil.

'Go on!' rasped Samuel Brevington peremptorily.

Belle gathered her thoughts together, gulped and continued, 'Abe turned on him an' hit him. Hard. Twice. Poor Willie was knocked backwards against the balustrade. Then Abe bent down an' grabbed him by the legs an' . . . an' . . . tossed him over.'

'I put it to you that he did no such thing,' remarked Brevington, 'that Willie Malone simply toppled over the rails as he attempted to pull himself upright. In other words, it was a pure accident.'

'No!'

'Tell me, Miss Busby, do you, in your chosen profession, often have occasion to tell lies?' The lawyer emphasized the words 'chosen profession' and at the same time stared meaningfully at the jury.

'Wa'al, er. . . .'

'Think carefully before you reply. Remember you are under oath.'

'I . . . I sometimes do.'

'Sometimes? I should think you do so frequently. Murmuring endearments you don't mean into your customer's ear, for instance.'

'That . . . that's not really lyin'.'

'No? Well, I suggest that you are lying now. Abe Fletcher had chosen to beat you up rather than admit to himself his shortcomings. Not something he

38

is now particularly proud of. But, at the time, he was full of beer. It was the act of a drunken young man, who was ashamed that his libido had failed. He took it out on you. And he hurt you badly. Two black eyes, a bloodied nose, a split lip and two cracked ribs, as well as various bruises and contusions. That is all in the doctor's report. Right?'

'Yes.'

'And, therefore, you are now extracting your revenge by lying. It is your earnest wish that my client should hang.'

'Yes, it is.'

'Ah, so you admit it!'

'Because he did murder Willie. For no other reason.'

'Huh! You are asking the jury to believe that?'

'I am, because it's true.'

'Yours is merely the evidence of an angry and immoral young woman who's clearly seeking vengeance.'

'No.'

'You are asking the jury to disbelieve Abe Fletcher, normally an upstanding young man and pillar of the community and, instead, take the word of a . . . a . . . what do you like to call yourself? . . . a "sporting woman",' he pronounced sarcastically.

'I am not lying.'

'But you have admitted that you lie to your customers as a matter of course.'

'I do not lie under oath.'

'No?'

'No. I would never lie under oath.'

Samuel Brevington cursed beneath his breath. When he had taken on the case, he had anticipated an easy victory. He had expected that he, an experienced and sophisticated big city lawyer, would easily intimidate a bunch of country hicks into speaking up for his client. And, as for the two who were prosecution witnesses, he had had no doubt that he would be able to destroy their credibility at the witness-box. However, he had certainly failed to do so in the case of Belle Busby.

Joe Dunn's trouble-shooter proved no easier to subdue and Brevington was quite unable to find any reason why he would lie: Vince Preston knew what he had seen and was not about to permit some Chicago smart-ass to persuade him otherwise. Once again, Abe Fletcher's counsel had to admit defeat.

It was, therefore, a somewhat chastened advocate who summed up for the defence. He made great play regarding the fact that Abe Fletcher was of previously good character, whereas Belle Busby and Vince Preston could hardly be considered as model citizens. But that was the best he could do. He could not claim that any of the many defence witnesses were prepared to state unequivocally that Abe Fletcher did not heave Willie Malone off the balcony. Neither could he claim that either of the two prosecution witnesses was prepared to retract his or her statement that he did.

Local man, Dan Elam, on the other hand, when he

summed up for the prosecution a few minutes earlier, was presented with a much easier task. He had sworn evidence to the effect that Willie Malone was killed deliberately. And he concluded thus: 'Finally, gentlemen of the jury, I would point out that the balcony's balustrade stands at exactly four foot and so, should someone of six foot or more stagger backwards into it, the top would strike him somewhere near the small of his back and, consequently, he could conceivably lose his balance and topple over it into the bar-room below. However, when I checked with the mortician, Mr Bartlby, I found that the late Willie Malone measures a mere five foot, two inches. I rest my case.'

As a deflated Brevington sat down, Elmer Atkins turned to the jury and instructed them to retire and consider the evidence laid before them, and arrive at their verdict. He concluded by warning them that, should they have any doubts whatsoever, they must return a verdict of 'Not Guilty'.

Robert Fletcher and his younger son sat with bowed heads, anxiously awaiting the jury's decision. Neither felt sanguine regarding the likely outcome. Both had listened intently to Abe when he was examined by the prosecuting counsel and denied intentionally heaving Willie Malone over the balustrade. Although neither would admit as much, they did not, in their heart of hearts, believe him. They knew he was lying to save his neck.

It seemed that the jury agreed with them for, less than twenty minutes later, they returned and the foreman announced that they had reached a unanimous verdict. He then pronounced Abe to be guilty.

Judge Elmer Atkins nodded grimly. He did not look at his old comrade-in-arms, but directed his gaze at the young figure in the dock.

'Abe Fletcher,' he said solemnly,' you have been found guilty of the heinous crime of murder. Usually, in such cases, the penalty is death by hanging. However, it is my considered opinion that, in this instance, there are extenuating circumstances.' He did not explain what they were, but simply stated, 'Therefore, I sentence you to ten years' imprisonment in the state penitentiary.'

This sentence was greeted by a gasp of amazement, looks of disbelief and, from those Snake Springs citizens seated in the courtroom, howls of rage interspersed with angry shouts:

'It's a darned disgrace!'

'The judge has been bought!'

'Hang the murderin' sonofabitch.'

Elmer Atkins made no attempt to restore order. He had repaid his debt to Robert Fletcher, but at some cost to his conscience, his integrity and his sense of justice. Without so much as a single glance in the direction of the rancher, he ordered that Abe Fletcher be taken down and then he left the courtroom.

Robert, meanwhile, remained with his head clutched in his hands. How on earth, he asked himself, could he tell his beloved Emily that their elder son was now a convicted murderer?

# SEPTEMBER 1889

# CHAPTER THREE

Bill Brannigan and his gang of outlaws had spent the last few months journeying across the states of Montana, Idaho and Wyoming. They would hide out near some cow-town, which Brannigan would then enter and survey. Should he be satisfied with what he had seen, the gang would ride in and rob the bank. In this manner, they had raided no fewer than ten banks so far.

A day earlier, the gang had ridden into Fremont County and approached the town of Ellis Creek. They had camped amongst the foothills of the Wind River Range while their leader rode into town. They were breakfasting beside their camp-fire when he returned. There were five of them altogether: Red Ned Davis, Hank Jolley, J.J. Jones, Fencepost Mulcahy and Seth Erickson, all dressed in grey Stetsons and long, brown, ankle-length leather coats. For weapons, each carried a Remington in his holster and a Winchester in his saddleboot. Bill Brannigan was similarly attired and armed.

Once he had dismounted and availed himself of a mug of coffee, Brannigan addressed the others.

'OK, boys,' he said. 'I've checked out Ellis Creek an' I reckon it'll be a push-over.'

'Is that so, Bill?' growled Red Ned Davis.

'It is, Ned. The Cattlemen's Bank is situated at one end of Main Street an' the law office is at the other. Bad plannin' from the town's point of view, but perfect from ours. We can be in an' outta that thar bank 'fore the marshal is half-way down Main Street. An' by the time he's summoned a posse, we'll be long gone.'

'Yippee! So, when do we hit this bank?' cried Hank Jolley.

'Jest as soon as we've drunk our coffee an' broken camp,' replied Brannigan.

He prayed that the Ellis Creek branch of the Cattlemen's Bank would hold a decent amount of cash, since the last three banks they had raided had held very small deposits indeed. Also, the gang's growing notoriety meant that the forces of law and order were out looking for them and quite likely already on their trail. What the gang needed to do urgently was divide up their illicit gains and then go their separate ways. Brannigan intended that he would ride south-west to sample the wild delights of 'Frisco. A successful and lucrative hold-up was therefore essential.

It took only a few minutes for the gang to get ready

to ride. With Bill Brannigan at their head and Red Ned Davis bringing up the rear, the six outlaws left their camp and set forth along the trail leading to Ellis Creek. They cantered towards the town and eventually entered it from the west. The bank was the third building they reached. But they were spotted as they halted and dismounted in front of it.

Brannigan was correct when he surmised that the forces of law and order were likely on his trail. US Marshal Guy Rogers had caught up with the gang almost immediately after their previous bank raid and had shadowed them to Ellis Creek. He had observed Bill Brannigan conduct his survey of the town and had guessed the outlaw chief's next move. Consequently, he had arranged for a reception party. Now he, together with town marshal Fred Somers and his deputies, Keith Riley and Matt Bacon, were hidden two doors down from the bank, in Terry Walters' general store. Also waiting there were Walters and several other of Ellis Creek's citizens, all heavily armed. From his vantage point at the window of the store, Marshal Fred Somers watched the outlaws climb the steps leading up on to the stoop. Only J.J. Jones remained below, as a look-out and in charge of their horses. The other five were carrying their saddle-bags and, moments later, they entered the bank.

'Them no-account critters have jest gone inside!' yelled Somers, and straightaway Marshal Rogers and the others tumbled out of the store into Main Street. Somers hastily followed.

Meanwhile, Bill Brannigan and his gang burst in upon the staff and customers of the Cattlemen's Bank, their revolvers drawn and ready to shoot.

Behind the counter, the manager, Lyle Granger, was consulting with his young cashier, Tim Newby. Both were dressed in dark grey three-piece suits, the former tall, elegant and imposing, the latter of medium height, young and fresh-faced.

In front of the counter stood two customers: Francie Pullen, a widow who owned the town's only dry goods store, and Phil Green, the proprietor of the local livery stables. Both were in their early fifties, the former dressed in a wide-brimmed straw hat and gingham dress, the latter in a faded check shirt and well-worn denims. Both were visiting the bank in order to deposit their previous day's takings.

The outlaws rushed inside brandishing their firearms, Francie screamed and the bank manager attempted to pull an ancient revolver from the shoulder-holster hidden beneath his jacket. But Lyle Granger was nowhere near quick enough on the draw. The gun had barely cleared his holster when Brannigan shot him. The bullet struck Granger in the chest and sent him crashing backwards to sprawl motionless on the floor, with a pool of blood slowly spreading out across his white shirt-front.

Francie continued to scream, while Tim Newby and Phil Green hastily stuck their hands in the air.

'Don't shoot! Don't shoot!' cried the young bank clerk.

'Wa'al, then, shuddup!' rasped Brannigan.

'Y . . . yessir!'

Brannigan grinned wolfishly and, turning to his confederates, yelled, 'OK, boys, fill them thar saddle-bags with as much loot as you can carry!'

As he spoke, the sound of a second shot echoed through the bank. This one came from the street and was immediately followed by Marshal Fred Somers shouting, 'Brannigan, you an' the rest of your gang come out with your hands up. We've got the bank surrounded!'

'Goddammit! How in tarnation..?' began the outlaw chief.

'They must've recognized you when you was givin' the town the once-over,' snarled Hank Jolley.

'Anyways, let's git the Hell outta here!' cried Red Ned Davis.

'Fill up your bags first,' snapped Brannigan.

'But. . . .' began Davis.

'Fill 'em up! Then we'll leave an' use these three as our hostages,' said Brannigan, indicating the bank clerk and the two customers with a jerk of his thumb.

'Yeah! That's smart thinkin',' commented Fencepost Mulcahy in admiration.

Consequently, a few minutes later, the outlaws and their hostages began slowly, nervously, to emerge through the bank's front door. As they did so, US Marshal Guy Rogers and town Deputy Matt Bacon entered the building from the rear.

'Drop your guns!' commanded Rogers.

Two of the outlaws whirled round to face this unexpected challenge. As they did so, one of the large crowd of lawmen and citizens, who had lined up in front of the bank, opened fire. Who it was, nobody afterwards was able to say. However, straight-away, everyone else opened up. The three hostages promptly dropped to the floor of the stoop and miraculously survived unscathed except for a few slight contusions.

Others were not so fortunate.

Inside the bank, US Marshal Guy Rogers swiftly shot Seth Erikson as he wheeled round, gun in hand. The slug struck the outlaw in the chest and penetrated his black heart. In the same instant, Fencepost Mulcahy returned fire. His first shot whistled past the marshal's left ear, but the second drilled a hole in the centre of the peace officer's forehead and exploded out of the back of his skull in a cloud of blood and brains. It was at this point that the young deputy, Matt Bacon, opened fire. No fewer than three slugs slammed into Mulcahy's body – two in the chest and one in the belly. Mulcahy slumped to the floor, where he lay barely breathing, while his life-blood slowly seeped away.

Outside the bank, J.J. Jones lay face downwards in the dust, close to where the gang's horses were teth-ered. Marshal Fred Somers had shot the robber as he and the others converged upon the bank. Indeed, the shot which had killed Jones was the same one that had alerted the outlaws inside.

During the course of the resulting gunfight in Main

Street, the outlaws escaped lightly. While four towns-folk were badly wounded, Red Ned Davis and Hank Jolley succeeded in mounting their horses and riding off quite unharmed. Although pursued by a hail of bullets, neither man was hit. They galloped across the town limits and off towards the mountains of the Wind River Range. Neither Davis nor Jolley had managed, however, to retain his saddle-bag. Not that this mattered much, since they had failed to cram more than a very small amount of banknotes into each.

The outlaws' leader, Bill Brannigan, was the only casualty the gang suffered during that brief gunfight outside the bank. He and Deputy Marshal Keith Riley had exchanged shots as Brannigan hurried down from the stoop and attempted to reach his horse. Brannigan was hit in the shoulder and knocked flat, while his shot whistled harmlessly over the deputy's head.

In the aftermath, as the local doctor tended to the four wounded citizens and the local mortician took care of the bodies of Marshal Rogers, Lyle Granger, and the three outlaws, Marshal Fred Somers and his two deputies escorted Bill Brannigan to the law office.

'When you've finished with them others, Doc, mebbe you'll come an' attend to this here sono-fabitch?' remarked Somers to the physician as he led Brannigan away.

'Certainly,' replied the doctor.

'I need tendin' now,' grumbled Brannigan, clutching his shoulder and wincing.

'You'll survive,' retorted Somers. 'Don't worry, I ain't gonna let you die. I'm gonna keep you alive right up until the minute we hang you.'

'So, git goin'!' rasped Deputy Keith Riley.

He had clapped a pair of handcuffs on to the robber's wrists and was propelling him none too gently towards the law office.

Once they reached it and stepped inside, Riley took Brannigan down a short corridor to where the cells lay and quickly shoved him into the nearest of them. Then the young deputy returned to the office, where he found Somers gathering up a sheaf of Wanted notices.

Somers pointed to one that featured an ugly, scar-faced individual.

'Brannigan!' he said. 'I recognized him straight-away from that livid white scar that runs from jest beneath his left eye to his jaw-bone. Now let's go identify the rest of 'em.'

The two peace officers made their way across Main Street to the funeral parlour. Half-way across, they encountered Deputy Matt Bacon and invited him to join them.

Inside the funeral parlour, mortician Brian Dunlop was tending to the body of Lyle Granger. The other four were laid out on marble slabs. As they passed that of Marshal Guy Rogers, the three lawmen removed their hats.

'Another good man gone,' murmured Somers grimly.

'Yeah,' responded the two deputies in unison.

'Wa'al, let's take a look at these three murderin' bastards,' said Somers, passing on to view the outlaws' corpses.

With the aid of the Wanted notices, they soon identified the three bodies as those of J.J. Jones, Fencepost Mulcahy and Seth Erikson.

'That leaves jest Red Ned Davis an' Hank Jolley,' commented the marshal.

'We gonna form a posse an' go after 'em?' asked Matt Bacon eagerly.

'Sure are,' said Somers. 'An' I'm gonna wire every goddam law officer within fifty miles of Ellis Creek to warn him to be on the look-out for the varmints. If'n' they stick together, they'll be spotted for certain.'

'How so?' enquired Keith Riley.

' 'Cause there ain't that many folks who are both bearded an' red-haired. Red Ned Davis is gonna stick out like a sore thumb.'

'An' Hank Jolley?' said Riley.

'He's a rough-lookin' sonofabitch, but he don't carry no distinguishin' features – scars an' the like. So, if'n' he parts company with Red Ned, he might jest git clean away.'

'Then let's hope he an' Red Ned continue to ride together,' said Bacon.

'Amen to that,' agreed Somers. 'Now, c'mon! We need to form that posse pronto.'

None of the three lawmen truly believed they would succeed in catching up with the fleeing bank robbers before they left Fremont County, yet they felt they had at least to try. It was their duty. They owed as much to the late Marshal Guy Rogers.

Meanwhile, Red Ned Davis and Hank Jolley rode on towards the distant mountains. Their aim was to put as many miles as possible between themselves and Ellis Creek before they exhausted their horses and were forced to stop for respite.

'Where are we makin' for?' asked Red Ned Davis, as they approached a fork in the trail. 'Do we take left or right?'

'Left,' replied Hank Jolley firmly.

'You got a reason?'

'Yeah – I've got me a cousin lives twenty, mebbe twenty-five miles west of here. He has a small homestead jest outside Calico City.'

'Never heard of it.'

'It's a small cow-town 'bout the same size as Ellis Creek. Anyways, I figure we could hide up there for a while. Till the hue an' cry dies down.'

'You can trust your cousin?'

'I reckon.' Hank Jolley turned in the saddle and faced his fellow fugitive. 'You have a better plan?' he enquired.

'Nope,' admitted Red Ned Davis.

'Then we head for Calico City. OK?'

'OK!'

The two riders promptly urged their mounts forward, down the left-hand fork.

# CHAPTER FOUR

At approximately the same time that the Brannigan gang were carrying out their raid on the Cattlemen's Bank in Ellis Creek, Abe Fletcher was being released from the State Penitentiary, having served his full ten years' sentence.

Waiting for him as he stepped through the prison gates were his father and brother. They were standing holding the reins of three horses: their own mounts and one that they had brought along for Abe to ride.

Abe made no attempt to embrace them, nor they him. All three looked decidedly uncomfortable.

'You ain't visited me in eight years. Not since you came to tell me Ma had died,' said Abe accusingly.

'That's right,' retorted Robert Fletcher, his features harsh and his gaze icy.

'Pa blames you for Ma's death,' explained Brett.

'Me?'

'You're darned tootin' I do!' declared the rancher.

55

Your ma took your bein' sent to prison for murder real bad. She was plumb devastated. Never got over it.'

'Yeah. The two times Ma came here to visit you she broke down. She was ill for days afterwards,' added Brett.

'Which is why I never brought her again,' said their father. Then he continued, 'She went into a decline. Couldn't bear the thought that her elder son was responsible for killin' that poor, inoffensive ole feller, Willie Malone. An' when she visited Snake Springs shortly after the killin', she found herself bein' shunned by folks who used to be her friends. That made matters even worse. She steered clear of the town after that. Withdrew into her shell an' slowly faded away. You killed her jest as surely as you did Willie Malone.'

'No! That ain't fair. I. . . .' began Abe angrily.

'Your ma died of a broken heart. An' you're the one who broke it,' stated Robert Fletcher flatly.

'What Pa says is true,' added Brett in a quiet tone devoid of all emotion.

Abe stared at his father and brother. Their failure to visit him for the last eight years of his prison sentence had conditioned him to expect a less than friendly reunion. Indeed, he had not been at all sure that they would be there to greet him when his sentence was completed and he was released from the prison. But here they were.

'If you feel like that – the both of you – why are you

here?' he demanded.

' 'Cause I need to tell you somethin',' said his father.

'Oh, yeah? An' what's that, Pa?'

'I'm gonna disinherit you. I aim to draw up a new will in which I shall leave everythin' to Brett.'

'Whaddya mean, everythin'?'

'The ranch an' any savin's I might have.'

'But I'm the older son! The ranch should be mine by right!'

'Wa'al, it ain't gonna be. You have lost that right. Brett got hisself hitched last year an' he an' his wife will inherit. That's my final word.'

'You can't do this to me!'

'I can an' I will.'

'But the Triple F. . . .'

'That, too, is gonna be changed.'

'Whaddya mean?'

'The name. At the same time as I draw up my new will, I shall re-name the ranch the Double F.'

'An' jest when do you propose to do this?' enquired Abe hotly.

'Tomorrow mornin'. Me an' Brett, we'll be goin' into town to fetch some supplies. I aim to call in at our lawyer's office while we're there. By noon Brett will be my new heir.'

'You ain't wastin' much time,' said Abe.

'That's right. I ain't,' stated his father.

Abe turned his gaze upon his younger brother.

'You've persuaded Pa to do this!' he shouted.

Brett shook his head.

'Nope. You got that wrong, Abe. Pa didn't need no persuasion.'

'No? Wa'al, I'll bet you didn't try to change his mind,' rasped Abe.

'There would've been no point. You know Pa when his mind's made up.'

'Brett had nuthin' to do with this. The truth is, I don't wanna see you after today. Nevertheless, I know your ma wouldn't have wanted me to cast you out an' leave you penniless. So, for her sake, I'm gonna present you with three thousand dollars in cash – enough to help you make a new start. You was always good with hosses. Mebbe you could buy some an' start up a hoss ranch?'

So saying, Robert Fletcher stretched up and removed a small canvas bag from inside one of his saddle-bags. He handed it to Abe, who opened it and peered into its interior. The bag was packed with one hundred dollar bills, thirty of them in total. Abe closed the bag and slipped it into his inside coat pocket.

'Ain't you gonna thank Pa?' asked Brett.

'Nope. He's denied me my rightful inheritance. This is the very least he could do.'

'Aw, c'mon, Abe . . .' began Brett.

'It's OK, Brett,' his father interrupted. 'I neither need nor want Abe's gratitude.'

'That's good, 'cause you ain't gittin' it,' said Abe.

Robert Fletcher nodded.

'Jest one other thing, Abe. Whatever you decide to do – start up a hoss ranch or embark on some other kinda business – I'd advise you not to try doin' it back in Bridger County.'

'Oh, yeah? So that there's no chance you'll see me again?' sneered Abe.

'As I've already said, I don't wanna see you after today. But that ain't the sole reason. Feelin's against you are still runnin' high. Most of Snake Springs' citizens feel you got off light. They figure you should've been hanged. You come back an' I reckon some of 'em might jest git together an' string you up.'

Abe Fletcher blanched. This was something he had not considered. He had assumed that, ten years on, the killing of Willie Malone would have been pretty much forgotten. Had he still been his father's heir, Abe would have taken his chances and returned to the ranch. However, in the present circumstances, he decided to take his father's advice. After all, how could he possibly launch a successful business with the majority of Bridger County's population against him?

'OK, you win,' he muttered.

' 'Bye, then!'

Robert stretched out his hand towards Abe, as did Brett. But Abe was having none of it. He ignored their gesture and turned and mounted the spare horse, which they had brought along for him to ride. They stood and watched as he settled himself in the saddle.

'Where's the nearest town?' he asked gruffly.

'That way – Calico City. It's 'bout ten miles along the trail,' replied Brett.

Abe made no response but immediately set off in the direction indicated by his younger brother.

The other two kept him in their sight until, eventually, he rounded a bend in the trail and disappeared. Thereupon, they mounted their horses and began the fifty-odd mile ride back to Bridger County and the soon-to-be Double F ranch.

The ten miles to Calico City were soon covered. Abe trotted across the town limits and rode slowly along Main Street until he reached its one and only bank, a branch of the First National. He pulled up his horse and dismounted. Then, having tethered the steed to the hitching-rail outside, Abe entered the bank.

Inside, he found he was the only customer. He approached the counter behind which stood a couple of cashiers. He planted himself opposite the nearer of the two.

'Good mornin', sir. Can I help you?' enquired the clerk.

'Sure can,' said Abe. 'I want one of these here hundred dollar bills changed into fives.'

Thereupon, he produced the small canvas bag from inside his coat and took out one of the thirty hundred dollar bills.

'You ain't one of our customers, are you, sir?'

asked the clerk.

'No, I ain't,' said Abe. 'But I'm thinkin' of openin' an account. However, 'fore I do, I've got me a li'l business needs attendin' to.'

The clerk glanced over his shoulder. The bank manager sat in his office with the door open. He had evidently heard all that had been said and he nodded in response to the clerk's unspoken question.

Immediately, the clerk removed a stack of five dollar bills from a drawer beneath the counter and counted out twenty, which he then exchanged for the note Abe had laid on the counter.

'There you are, sir,' he said, as he gathered up the bills and handed them to Abe.

'Thank you,' said Abe.

Abe had no intention of depositing any of his cash with the bank, since he did not expect to be staying long in Calico City. But he guessed that, by pretending to be a prospective customer, he would have no trouble changing one of his large notes into smaller denominations. Smiling broadly, Abe Fletcher left the bank.

Having obtained directions from the bank clerk, he made his way down the street to the general store, where he intended purchasing a revolver, a holster, a rifle and a saddleboot. Then he proposed to stable his horse, engage a room for the night and go find the nearest saloon. A decade had passed since he had last sampled a beer and Abe was eager to remedy that situation.

It was just as Abe found and entered the general store that another stranger rode into town.

This second stranger was none other than the famous Kentuckian gunfighter, Jack Stone. Six foot two inches in his bare feet, Stone consisted of nigh on two hundred pounds of muscle and bone. He was pretty darned quick for a big man, though slow to anger. However, when riled, he displayed the ferocity that had earned him the name of being half-mountain lion and half-grizzly bear. The years had taken their toll, though, leaving scars both mental and physical. His square-cut, deeply lined face had been handsome once and, now and again when he smiled, it regained something of its former good looks.

It was through circumstances rather than inclination that Jack Stone had become a rover. Born the son of a Kentucky farmer, he most likely would still have been farming the family homestead had not his father been forced to sell it to pay his gambling debts. Shortly afterwards, his father had been killed in a saloon brawl. Thereafter, the widow had struggled, alone and unaided, to bring up her young son. Stone was fourteen years old when, worn out by her efforts, his mother, too, had died. From then onward, he had been on his own.

Stone had tried most things: farm work, ranch work, riding herd on several cattle drives, a little bronco-busting, even a spell working the gold mines of Colorado. Then, with the advent of the Civil War, he had fought for the Union and, afterwards for a while, served as an army scout. But the white man's savagery towards the native tribes had sickened Stone and he had resigned.

Later, he had taken on a job as a ranch-hand in Nevada and met and married Mary Spencer, a local storekeeper's daughter. He intended to sink his roots, but it was not to be for, within a year, Mary died in childbirth, with the child stillborn. This tragic event had a devastating effect on him, and it was some months before he recovered. He was, by then, a changed man: a man who would always be moving on, always looking for another frontier to cross.

His reputation as a gunfighter had been earned subsequently, with a series of jobs as stagecoach guard, deputy US marshal, deputy sheriff and, most famously, sheriff of Mallory – the roughest, toughest town in the state of Colorado. Indeed, it was as the man who tamed Mallory that he had become a legend of the West.

Now, he rode his bay gelding down Main Street, a tall, broad-shouldered figure attired in a grey Stetson, grey shirt, knee-length buckskin jacket, faded denim pants and unspurred boots. Around his strong, thick neck he wore a red kerchief and on his right thigh he carried a Frontier Model Colt tied down.

As he drew level with the Silver Dollar Saloon, Stone spied a woman coming out through the batwing doors. Although she was a few years older than when he had last encountered her, the

Kentuckian recognized her straightaway. She was a petite bottle-blonde, by now in her early forties, pretty rather than beautiful, with mischievous brown eyes, an upturned nose and a perpetually cheeky grin. She was wearing a neat blue cotton dress that fell in full flare to her ankles and she was carrying a heavy-looking portmanteau in one hand and a hatbox in the other.

'Wa'al, if it ain't my old acquaintance, Arizona Audrey!' exclaimed Stone.

The woman looked up in surprise. Then, as she in turn recognized him, her features split into a wide, beaming smile.

'Jack! Jack Stone!' she cried.

Stone leapt out of the saddle, while Arizona Audrey promptly laid down her portmanteau and hatbox. Then she threw herself into the Kentuckian's arms and they embraced and kissed.

'So, how're you doin', Audrey?' asked Stone when, presently, they came up for air.

'I've jest been sacked,' said Audrey bitterly.

Stone glanced towards the saloon.

'You was engaged to sing there?' he growled.

'Yup. But I ain't as young as I once was an' I've been replaced by a group of twenty-three-year-olds. Guess that's show-business.'

'You wanna tell me all about it?'

'Yeah. I could sure use a sympathetic ear.'

'Wa'al, I'm aimin' to book into that thar hotel,' said Kentuckian, pointing at the Alhambra, which stood directly opposite the saloon on the other side of the street. 'If'n' you ain't got no definite plans, you might care to join me?'

' 'Deed I would, Jack,' said Arizona Audrey.

'OK. Let me hitch my hoss to that rail an' then I'll help you with your baggages.'

'Thank you, Jack.'

Stone smiled, then led his bay gelding across Main Street and secured it to the hotel's hitching-rail. Thereupon, he picked up Audrey's portmanteau. She, for her part, retrieved the hatbox and linked arms with the big man, whereupon the pair headed for the Alhambra and disappeared inside.

They found themselves in a narrow lobby at the end of which was a small reception desk. Behind this desk stood a thin, bald-headed, bespectacled clerk.

'I'd like to book a room,' said Stone.

'For how long, sir?' enquired the clerk.

'I ain't sure. For tonight certainly. I'll let you know tomorrow mornin' if we intend stayin' longer.'

'Very good, sir.' The clerk got him to sign the hotel register, requested a deposit and then handed Stone a door-key. 'If you require lunch, we shall be servin' in 'bout one hour from now. The restaurant's there an' the bar-room's next-door,' he added, indicating two doors leading off the lobby.

'Room Number Seven,' said Stone, as he studied the label attached to the large iron key.

'Yessir. First door on your right at the head of the stairs. It overlooks Main Street,' explained the clerk.

'Thanks.'

Stone led the way upstairs and let them into the room. It was basic, but clean. Both of them noted, with some satisfaction, the large double-bed. They dumped the portmanteau on the floor and the hatbox on a chair.

'What about your belongin's?' said Audrey.

Stone grinned.

'I travel light. My few things are in my saddle-bags. Guess I'll bring 'em up later when I go tend to my hoss. Then mebbe we'll have ourselves a drink in the bar-room followed by lunch?'

'Sounds good, Jack. An' for now?'

'I wanna hear what you've been up to since we parted company in Flagstaff. When was it, six years back?'

'I reckon.'

'Wa'al, did you head back to Bonnie Springs like you said you would?'

'Sure did. An' I stayed there till a coupla years back when Frenchie retired an' went south to New Orleans, from where she originally hailed. You remember Frenchie?'

Stone nodded. At the time he had been involved in hunting down a gang of ruthless bank-robbers led by the notorious J.C. Sharkey. During the course of that particular adventure, he had encountered Arizona Audrey in the small Nevada town of Bonnie Springs. She and four scantily-clad young brunettes had provided the entertainment at Frenchie's Place,

Audrey singing and the other four executing a none-too-expert dance routine. Unluckily for her, Audrey had inadvertently got caught up in the hunt for J.C. Sharkey and his confederates, and had ended up in Flagstaff where the gang finally met their doom. However, during the course of that adventure, she and Stone had enjoyed a short, yet extremely passionate, relationship. Then he had headed south and she, it seemed, had made her way back to Bonnie Springs and resumed her singing career at Frenchie's Place.

'So you remained singin' at Frenchie's Place for another four years?' said Stone.

'Yup. Then, like I said, Frenchie retired. She sold the saloon to some lunkhead who promptly changed its name an' sacked me an' Les Girls. Reckoned we was old hat. Like George Young, the owner of the Silver Dollar across the street, he was lookin' for younger performers to entertain his customers.'

'You still look pretty darned good to me, Audrey.'

'Thanks, Jack. Unfortunately, Mr Young don't seem to agree with you.'

'More fool he.'

'Yeah, wa'al, it's his saloon an', so, here I am no longer in employment. You don't know anyone who's lookin' for an out-of-work saloon singer, do you?'

'Not off-hand. But, tell me, what have you been doin' since you left Frenchie's Place? Did you come straight here to the Silver Dollar?'

Audrey shook her head.

'Nope. Me an' *Les Girls*, we split up an' I went solo. I worked my way through a string of saloons an' tin-pot theatres across Nevada an' Utah an' up into Wyomin'. Finally, I reached this one-horse town an' have been singin' at the Silver Dollar since July.'

'I see.'

'But I'm beginnin' to think that mebbe my days as a songstress are over. Reckon I'll ditch my stage name. Goodbye, Arizona Audrey. From now on I'll be jest plain Audrey.'

'That's one thing you ain't – plain!' Stone grinned and pulled the blonde into his arms. 'Goddammit, you're still one hell of an attractive women!' he exclaimed, as he kissed her.

Audrey responded and, kissing and caressing each other with rapidly growing desire, the pair began hurriedly to undress. The sight of the blonde's small, firm breasts roused the Kentuckian's passions to fever-pitch and, moments later, they were both stark naked and sprawled across the large double-bed.

'Oh, yes! Yes! Yes!' she cried as the Kentuckian mounted her.

# CHAPTER FIVE

In the aftermath of their lovemaking, Jack Stone and Audrey relaxed together in the double-bed. During the course of his wanderings across the West, Stone had bedded several women, mostly sporting women, and each time moved on without regret. Since the tragic death of his wife, he had felt he could never love another woman as he had loved her. And, on the previous occasion he had encountered Audrey, while enjoying her favours, Stone had not considered the possibility of their ever forming a permanent relationship. Now, six years later, the Kentuckian felt somewhat differently. This chance meeting might, he thought to himself, be the beginning of something good, something lasting. He turned to the blonde, kissed her and was about to broach the subject when he was interrupted by the sounds of a commotion outside in Main Street.

'What in tarnation. . . ?' he exclaimed.

'Let's go look,' said Audrey, her curiosity roused.

They hastily clambered off the bed and went across to the window, crouching down so that anyone glancing up from the street would see only their heads. Neither of them wished to flaunt their nakedness before the gaze of Calico City's populace.

Opposite the hotel stood the Silver Dollar Saloon, and next to it the law office. A crowd was forming in front of the law office and, as Stone and Audrey watched, a young deputy marshal emerged from the saloon followed by its proprietor and several of his customers. Within a couple of minutes, most of Calico City's citizenry were gathered there. Then the door of the law office opened and Marshal Dave Grant stepped outside on to the sidewalk.

Dave Grant was a man in his early thirties, a tough, single-minded character, who, in his five years as town marshal, had changed a wild and well-nigh lawless cattle-town into a respectable, safe and fast-expanding county seat. He was both liked and respected by the townsfolk and, in his black Stetson and smart Prince Albert coat, he cut a tall, elegant figure, as he stood there on the sidewalk facing the crowd. He raised his hand and began to speak.

As he did so, the Kentuckian leant forward and pushed open the window in order that he and Audrey might hear what the peace officer had to say.

'Fellow citizens,' shouted the marshal, 'I have jest received a wire from my opposite number in Ellis Creek, Marshal Fred Somers. In it he informs me that the notorious Brannigan gang hit town this very morning.' This brought forth a variety of gasps and cries from amongst his listeners. He waited for the hubbub to die down and then continued, 'But there is good news. The gang's raid on the bank there failed, Bill Brannigan was shot, wounded and captured, an' three of his confederates were shot dead.'

'But I understood there were five of 'em in Brannigan's gang!' cried a short, fat man, who was dressed in a frock coat and tall stovepipe hat and stood at the front of the crowd.

'Exactly, Mr Mayor,' replied Grant.

'Then, what's happened to the other two?' demanded the fat man.

'I was about to explain. They escaped an', accordin' to Marshal Somers, were headin' this way. Red Ned Davis an' Hank Jolley. A coupla desperate characters who must be apprehended. Marshal Somers is formin' a posse an' givin' chase. He states he has alerted every law officer within fifty miles of Ellis Creek, so you can be sure there'll be plenty of other posses settin' out to look for 'em.'

'We lie 'bout twenty-five miles west of Ellis Creek,' commented the mayor.

'Yup. Which is why I got my deppities to call you all together. I, too, aim to form a posse an' go lookin' for them two no-account murderin' critters. So, how's about volunteerin', folks?'

This request brought forth a chorus of offers.

Jack Stone turned to face Audrey.

'I gotta go,' he said quietly.

The blonde frowned.

'But why, Jack? There's plenty other volunteers an'. . . .'

'Earlier, you told me how you happened to be in Calico City. But I didn't say what brought me here.'

'So, what did bring you to Calico City?' she asked.

'Some while back, a good friend of mine was shot in the back an' killed. At the time he was ridin' home to his ranch from town, where he'd been fetchin' supplies. Anyhow, he was bushwhacked by a road-agent who'd been lyin' in wait for unsuspectin' travellers. That road-agent's name is Red Ned Davis.'

'How . . . how'd you know? If'n' your friend was shot in the back an' killed. . . .'

'A coupla cowpokes from a neighbourin' ranch had been to town on a similar errand. They weren't far behind my friend an' they rounded a bend in the trail an' witnessed the whole thing.' Stone frowned and added, 'Unfortunately, they were ridin' a buckboard an', so, were unable to pursue the murderin' sonofabitch, who, of course, was on horseback.'

'But they were sure the killer was Red Ned Davis?'

'Oh, yeah! That red beard of his is a give-away. An' I've been trackin' him down ever since. A few months back, I learned he'd taken up with the Brannigan gang, who'd lately been rampagin' through these parts. I've been tryin' to catch up with 'em for quite some time, as, I guess, has the law.'

'It's a pity Red Ned Davis didn't git his comeuppance durin' that raid on the bank in Ellis Creek.'

'Wa'al, he didn't, so I'm afraid I gotta go.'

'Oh, Jack, you will be careful? Don't go takin' no unnecessary risks,' cried Audrey.

Stone smiled. The concern written on the blonde's face was plain to see. He was touched.

'I'll be careful,' he promised.

'Be sure you are.'

'You'll be here when I return?' he growled.

'I ain't got me no plans to move on yet awhile. So, I'll be here, waitin' for you, Jack,' declared Audrey.

The Kentuckian pulled her close and they embraced and kissed. Then, they parted and hurriedly began to dress.

A few minutes later, both were fully attired. They kissed one last time and then Stone said, 'Let's go.'

He opened the hotel door and, as he did so, the door to the room next-door was also thrust open. Abe Fletcher stepped out into the corridor that divided the rooms overlooking Main Street from those looking out over the hotel's stables at the rear. Abe had taken the room, following his visit to the general store, and, having examined it, was now on his way to enjoy a few beers at the Silver Dollar Saloon.

' 'Mornin',' he said, doffing his Stetson to Audrey.

' 'Mornin',' replied the blonde.

Stone added his greeting and they followed Abe Fletcher downstairs and out into the street. Abe, too, had heard Marshal Dave Grant's plea for volunteers to join his posse, but he had not the slightest intention of enlisting. He headed straight for the saloon.

Audrey stood with the crowd gathered in the street outside the law office, while Stone stepped up on to the sidewalk and greeted the marshal.

' 'Mornin', Marshal, I'd sure like to ride with you,' he said.

Grant carefully studied the big, tough-looking stranger who confronted him. He reckoned that here was a man he would rather have on his side than against him.

'Wa'al, you seem the kinda feller I'm lookin' for. My name's Dave Grant, by the way. An' you are. . . ?' he asked, as he continued to run his eye over the big man.

'Stone. Jack Stone,' replied the Kentuckian.

The marshal's eyebrows raised in an expression of surprise.

'Gee! It's a pleasure to meet you, Mr Stone,' he declared.

'You've heard of me, then?' said Stone.

'Sure have! You've got one helluva reputation. What are you doin' in these parts?'

'I'm on the trail of Red Ned Davis.'

'For the bounty?'

'Nope. I ain't no bounty hunter.'

'Then. . . ?'

'Davis shot a friend of mine.' Stone paused and added, 'In the back.'

'I see.'

'So, I'd 'preciate joinin' your posse, if'n' you'll

have me.'

'An' if I don't?'

'I'll go lookin' for him anyway.'

'In that case, you'd best join the posse.'

'Thanks. I'll go git my hoss.'

' 'Fore you do, let me introduce you to my two deppities.' Grant turned to the two young men flanking him. 'Walter Coburn an' Nick O'Brien. Boys, meet the famous Kentuckian gunfighter, Jack Stone.'

'Pleased to meet you, Mr Stone,' said an awestruck Coburn.

'Yessir,' added O'Brien enthusiastically.

'Pleased to meet you boys,' replied Stone and, having shaken hands with the three peace officers, he crossed the street and unhitched his bay gelding from the rail outside the Alhambra Hotel.

Audrey left the crowd still standing in front of the law office and went over to greet him.

'Wa'al, that's it, then. You've enlisted.'

'Yup.'

Stone gathered the blonde into his arms and kissed her. Then he released her, stepped back and swiftly mounted his horse. He raised his hand in a farewell gesture.

'Be seein' you, Audrey,' he said.

'I sure hope so, Jack,' said the blonde.

They smiled at each other, whereupon Stone wheeled the gelding round and trotted off to join the marshal and his two deputies, who, by this time, had mounted their horses in readiness for departure.

Several others rode up and eventually, excluding Stone and the three peace officers, the posse numbered seventeen. The fat mayor, eleven townsfolk and five homesteaders had volunteered to ride.

'So, which way do we head?' enquired the mayor.

'The wire I received from Ellis Creek stated that Red Ned Davis and Hank Jolley were headin' in this direction,' said Marshal Grant. 'That means they're comin' from the east.'

'An' I guess they won't have had time to reach here yet,' said Deputy Coburn.

'That's right, Walter. Therefore, I figure we ride out to meet 'em.'

So saying, the marshal dug his heels into his horse's flanks and set off eastward along Main Street in the direction of the neighbouring Fremont County. The rest of the posse followed in his wake and, as they crossed the town limits and hit the main trail, they broke into a canter.

Stone rode more in hope than expectation. Red Ned Davis and Hank Jolley might have been heading west when they left Ellis Creek, but that did not mean they had continued to do so once they were out of sight of the town. They could have veered off in any direction they pleased: north, south or east. And, even had they remained riding westward, they need not have stuck to the main trail. There were many roundabout routes that could be taken, either to reach Calico City or to circumvent it. Nevertheless, Stone stayed with Marshal Dave Grant and his posse

76

and kept his eyes peeled for any sign of the two fugitives. He could think of no alternative course of action and it was just possible, if not probable, that the posse and the outlaws might meet head-on.

Meantime, back in Calico City, the crowd, having cheered Marshal Grant and his men on their way, began to disperse. Some returned to their homes and others to their places of work or business. Quite a number of the menfolk did neither but, instead, trooped into George Young's Silver Dollar Saloon.

Audrey, for her part, returned to the hotel. She had had no breakfast that morning and, therefore, was beginning to feel extremely hungry. She recalled the reception clerk's words and made straight for the hotel restaurant.

# CHAPTER SIX

Homesteader Vic Morgan was amongst those who entered the Silver Dollar following the departure of the posse.

A small, lean individual, a bachelor in his late thirties, though looking older, Morgan was pretty much worn out from scratching a living on the homestead that he had rented and lived upon for the last decade. A thin, weather-beaten and much lined face peered out from beneath a badly battered and frayed Stetson. His check shirt was threadbare, his blue denims faded and worn and his boots scuffed and down at heel.

Morgan did not carry a hand-gun. And he had not rallied to the marshal's call to arms. Instead, he had been one of the first to enter the saloon at the conclusion of Grant's oration. He felt in sore need of a stiff drink, since one of the two wanted men, Hank Jolley, happened to be his cousin.

Abe Fletcher was not far behind the homesteader

and found a space next to him at the bar-counter. He arrived as Morgan hastily threw back a whiskey in one gulp and then proceeded to half-empty his glass of beer. Abe watched in admiration.

'You sure got a thirst on you!' he exclaimed.

Morgan turned to face the newcomer and smiled.

'Yeah, guess I have at that,' he replied, before consuming the rest of the beer in a single draught.

'May I buy you another?' asked Abe, who, as a stranger in town and recently abandoned by his family, was anxious for a little friendly company.

'That's mighty civil of you, sir,' replied Morgan. 'Jest a beer this time.'

'Right.'

Abe caught the eye of one of George Young's bartenders and ordered two beers. Then he introduced himself to the homesteader.

'Abe Fletcher.'

'Vic Morgan.'

The pair shook hands. Thereupon, Abe paid for the beers and they both lifted their glasses and drank.

'Shall we take a seat?' asked Abe, as he lowered his glass.

'Yeah. Why not?' said the other.

They found an empty table in a corner of the saloon and sat down.

'You live in these parts?' enquired Abe.

'Yup. I've got me a homestead 'bout a quarter of a mile outside town. But you're a stranger.'

'Yeah.'

'So, what brought you to Calico City?'

'It's a long story.'

'Wa'al, I ain't goin' nowhere in a hurry. Therefore, if you wanna bend my ear. . . ?'

Abe, still angry at losing what he considered to be his birthright, was only too willing to get the matter off his chest. Indeed, he craved a sympathetic ear and he reckoned that Vic Morgan might be just the man to provide one.

'I've jest, this very day, been released from jail,' he confessed.

Vic Morgan whistled softly in surprise.

'How long did you serve?' he asked.

'Ten years.'

Again Vic Morgan whistled softly.

'What did you do to warrant that long a sentence?'

'I killed a man.' And, not wishing to lose the other's sympathy, he added, 'It was an accident, but the court didn't see it that way.'

'No?'

'No.'

'So, what now? You figurin' on stayin' here in Calico City or are you headin' home?'

Abe shook his head.

'I ain't got me no home. Not any more.'

'How come?'

So, Abe told Morgan of how his father and brother had been waiting outside the prison when he was released. Then, he went on to tell him that his father was proposing to disinherit him in favour of his younger brother and had warned him against returning to Bridger County.

'That's terrible,' said Morgan. 'You mean to say your father has left you with nuthin'?'

'Not exactly nuthin'.'

'Whaddya mean?'

'He's paid me off, I guess you could say.'

'Paid you off? How much, if I ain't bein' too nosey?'

'Three thousand dollars.'

Once again Vic Morgan whistled softly.

'That's one helluva lot of loot,' he commented.

'You compare it to the ranch I should've inherited, the biggest an' best spread in the whole of Bridger County, an' that sum is little more'n a pittance.'

'A pittance I'd be happy to have,' thought Morgan, though he simply said, 'Yeah. Wa'al, you got my commiserations.'

'Thanks.'

'So, what are you aimin' to do?'

'I dunno. Pa said I could mebbe use the three thousand dollars to start me a hoss ranch some place.'

'But you ain't gonna do that?'

'Like I said, I dunno. I'm thinkin' about it.'

'An' meantime. . . ?'

'While I consider my next move, I'm stayin' across the street at the Alhambra.'

'I see.' Morgan smiled, finished his beer and said,

'Here, it's my turn to buy you a beer. OK?'

'Yeah. Thanks.'

Morgan rose and went across to the bar-counter, where he ordered two more beers. While he waited for the bartender to pour them, he considered the situation in which he found himself. He was barely scratching a living and had just struck up an acquaintance with a man who had been handed three thousand dollars as a pay-off. Abe Fletcher might regard that amount as a pittance; Vic Morgan most certainly did not. He determined to cultivate Abe while the other remained in Calico City. Perhaps he could devise some means of parting the stranger with a portion of those three thousand dollars? He paid for the beers and returned to join Abe at the corner table.

'So,' he said, after they had each swallowed a copious draught, 'when does your father propose to disinherit you? Is there no way you can persuade him to change his mind?'

Abe shook his head and scowled.

'No,' he said. 'Pa ain't gonna change his mind.'

'But surely you've gotta try to persuade. . . ?'

'There ain't no time. It's too late.'

'Whaddya mean?'

'Pa told me that tomorrow mornin', when he an' Brett ride into Snake Springs to fetch supplies, they're gonna call in on our lawyer an' he's gonna alter his will in Brett's favour. He said Brett will be his heir by noon tomorrow.'

'Ah!'

'I gotta accept it. I've lost the ranch.'

'Yeah.'

'So, for the present, I'm stayin' put here in Calico City.'

'Wa'al, as I've already said, you've got my commiserations. An' if'n' you need some company, I'll be happy to join you for a few beers.'

'Thanks. I guess I do need someone to talk to, mebbe bounce a few ideas off.'

'Then, I'm your man.'

'OK. After I've drunk this beer, I'm goin' back to the hotel to git myself somethin' to eat an' then quietly think things over. But I aim to return here this evenin' for a few beers. Mebbe we can meet then?'

'Yeah. I've got me a few chores to take care of this afternoon, so that'll suit me fine. You can bounce your ideas off me this evenin'.'

'OK.'

The two men chatted inconsequentially while they finished their beers. Then they left the saloon. Outside, they shook hands and went their separate ways. Abe Fletcher headed across the street and disappeared through the front door of the Alhambra Hotel, while Vic Morgan set off down Main Street in the direction of his homestead.

The distance between the Silver Dollar and the edge of town was approximately a quarter of a mile, and a further quarter-mile took him to the boundary of his farm. Morgan had chosen to walk this short way into town, since it would have taken nearly as long to hitch his ancient mule to his equally ancient buckboard as it did to cover the distance on foot.

And, while he trudged homeward, he continued to ponder how he might persuade his new acquaintance to include him in his plan. He was both weary of, and despondent regarding, his life as an impoverished homesteader. He had originally come out West in order to fashion a new life for himself, but the land he rented was poor and, although he was loathe to admit it even to himself, he was no farmer. Consequently, since arriving in Calico City ten years earlier, he had struggled to make ends meet.

His cousin, Hank Jolley, had accompanied him on the journey West and had taken a homestead next to his. However, Jolley had soon given up the land and gone his separate way, taking to a life of crime. Morgan had heard tales of his doings from time to time, as news of Jolley's infamy spread. Then, that very day, he had listened to Marshal Dave Grant and learned that his cousin was one of the two outlaws who had survived Brannigan's bank raid in Ellis Creek and escaped westward.

Therefore, in addition to thinking about Abe Fletcher and his three thousand dollars, Morgan could not prevent himself speculating on where Hank Jolley was headed. Could his bandit cousin be making for Calico City? Vic Morgan sincerely hoped not.

84

Thoughts about both were buzzing through Morgan's brain as he turned off the trail outside the town and proceeded up the rough path through the badly tended farm-land to his homestead. This was comprised of a rather ramshackle dwelling-house with stables and a small barn located immediately behind it. He reached the front door, which was unlocked, and thrust it open. Inside was a large, sparsely-furnished living-room-cum-kitchen and seated at the kitchen table were two men. Vic Morgan's worst fears had been realized. Hank Jolley and Red Ned Davis sat there, drinking his coffee.

'Hank! What in tarnation are you doin' here?' he demanded.

Hank Jolley scowled darkly. Both he and Red Ned Davis had removed their long, brown, ankle-length leather coats, but not their Stetsons.

'That don't sound too friendly, Vic. Ain't you pleased to see me?' growled Jolley.

Morgan shook his head, his face lined with worry.

'No,' he said. 'It's known that you an' your pal are on the lam after tryin' to hold up the bank in Ellis Creek. S'pose some of the folks round here recall you're my cousin? Hell, you farmed the land next door!'

'For 'bout six, seven months. That's all. An' the town was still growin' in those days. Folks comin' an' goin' all the time. Don't expect anybody remembers me now.'

'Mebbe not, but we can't be sure. If'n' someone

85

does an' mentions the fact to the marshal, he'll be certain to investigate.'

'Nobody's remembered so far,' interjected Red Ned Davis.

'How'd you know?' rasped Morgan.

'Wa'al, some li'l time back, when we was a coupla miles short of here, Hank an' me took cover an' watched what looked like a posse head thataway.' Davis stared out of one of the windows towards the trail that ran eastward past the homestead towards distant Fremont County. 'It was led by a feller I took to be the town marshal.'

'Yeah, you're right,' conceded Morgan.

'There you are, then,' said Davis. 'Evidently, nobody's suggested to him that Hank might be hidin' out here.'

'That don't mean nobody won't in the future,' said Morgan pessimistically.

'We ain't plannin' on stayin' here indefinitely,' said Jolley.

'Hmm.' Morgan frowned. 'Where are your hosses, by the way?' he asked.

'We curried an' fed 'em, an' stabled 'em out back,' replied his cousin.

'I see.'

'We also need feedin' an' restin' 'fore we move on,' remarked Davis.

Morgan brightened a little at hearing this. Perhaps they would have departed before anyone *did* recall his relationship to Hank Jolley?

'I guess I can knock you up a quick meal,' he said.

'Thanks. That's more like it, Vic,' commented Jolley.

'Sure is,' said Davis, smiling.

'But, first, I need a drink,' stated the homesteader.

'What kinda drink? A li'l coffee?' said Jolley.

'Nope. Whiskey.'

'Now you're talkin'!' beamed Red Ned Davis.

Morgan went and fetched a bottle of cheap rye whiskey and three glasses from a nearby cupboard and brought them over to the table where his cousin and Red Ned Davis were sitting. He poured three generous measures and raised his glass.

'Your health, Hank!' he proposed. 'An' yours, Ned,' he added, for, although his cousin hadn't mentioned his confederate's name, Marshal Grant had when he was recruiting his posse.

'You ain't exactly prosperin' here, are you, Vic?' said Jolley, as he lowered his glass.

'Nope.'

'You should've followed my example an' given up your homesteadin'. You ain't no more cut out to be a farmer than I am.'

'Mebbe not.'

'No "mebbe" about it. Me an' Ned might be on the run, but we still got prospects.'

'More banks to rob?' said Morgan, a sarcastic edge to his words.

'Next time we'll make sure we git what we're after. It was a mistake teamin' up with that lunkhead, Bill

Brannigan,' said Davis.

'Sure was,' agreed Jolley.

'So, you got any plan fixed?' enquired Morgan.

'Not yet. We're jest aimin' to git as far away from Ellis Creek as we can. What about you, Vic? You gonna stay here for the rest of your life?'

'Mebbe. Mebbe not.'

'Whaddya mean?'

'Wa'al, Hank, I encountered a stranger in town 'fore I came home, an' what he told me has set me thinkin'.'

'An' what exactly did this feller tell you?'

'He told me he was jest this mornin' released from prison after servin' ten years for murder.'

'Holy cow!'

'He reckoned it was an accident, but the jury didn't believe him.'

'Do you?'

'Dunno, Hank. Anyways, on his release, he was met at the prison gates by his pa and his brother. An' guess what they informed him?'

'How the Hell should I know? Spit it out, Vic.'

'They informed him that he was to be disinherited. Seems his pa owns the biggest an' best ranch in the whole of Bridger County, an' he's gonna make his younger son heir an' disinherit my acquaintance who happens to be the elder.'

Hank Jolley whistled through his teeth and took another gulp of his whiskey.

'That's kinda harsh on your pal,' he commented.

'He ain't my pal. Not yet, but I'm workin' on it,' said Morgan.

'Why bother?' asked Davis curiously.

' 'Cause his pa ain't left him entirely penniless.'

'No?' said Jolley.

'No, indeed! He's given him no less than three thousand dollars as a kinda pay-off.'

'Some pay-off! Wow!' Jolley regarded his cousin with a speculative eye. 'So, that's what's got you thinkin', eh? You're considerin' how to git your hands on some, or all, of that loot.'

'I sure am.'

'You could lure the sucker out here an' bump him off,' suggested Davis.

Morgan shook his head.

'No, I guess not,' he muttered.

'Vic don't even tote a gun.' Jolley glanced at the far wall, on which was hung an ancient shotgun. 'Less you count that,' he said, nodding at the firearm.

'That's purely there as a precaution, in case somebody tries to break in an'. . . .'

The homesteader's words were interrupted by a burst of raucous laughter from both Hank Jolley and Red Ned Davis.

'Who in tarnation's gonna bother to break in here?' asked Jolley when, eventually, he stopped laughing.

'I dunno? It . . . it's possible.'

'But highly unlikely.' Davis glanced at the shotgun. 'I take it the shotgun's loaded?'

'Yeah.'

'Then, you could use it to shoot him.'

'Told you, Ned, that ain't Vic's style,' said Jolley. 'But we could shoot him for you, Vic,' he stated eagerly.

'An' split the three thousand dollars between us,' added Davis.

'That's supposin' Abe's carryin' it around with him,' said Morgan.

'Abe?'

'Abe Fletcher. That's his name. Like I said, he left prison this mornin'. So, he could easily have deposited all, or at least some, of the three thousand dollars in the bank. There's a branch of the First National in Calico City's Main Street.'

'Why would he do that?' enquired Jolley.

'For safety's sake. He's a stranger in town an' that's a lotta loot to keep on his person.'

'Hmm. I s'pose.'

'Then, 'fore you invite him out here, mebbe you'd best find out what he's done with the money,' said Davis.

Morgan shook his head and frowned.

'No, I don't think so. If I try that, I might make him suspicious. Also, he's stayin' at the Alhambra. If'n' he disappears, Frank Humble, who owns the hotel, is gonna be lookin' for him. Abe Fletcher ain't sure how long he's gonna stay in town, so I figure he will have paid only a deposit for that room. Frank Humble will sure as dammit want what's left owin'.'

'He'll assume that Fletcher has jest upped an' left town,' said Davis.

'Not with his hoss still in the hotel stables, he won't.'

'Ah!'

'Into the bargain, I've been seen drinkin' an' talkin' with Abe an', anyways, how am I s'posed to bring him out here without nobody spottin' us? George Young, for one, don't miss much.'

'So much for that idea, then. You don't lure Mr Fletcher out here an' we don't kill him,' concluded Jolley.

'No.' Morgan sighed and said, 'What irks me is that Abe regards the three thousand dollars as a mere pittance.'

'A pittance?'

'Yeah, Hank. Not what I'd call that kinda money. But Abe reckons that, compared to the ranch which he was s'posed to inherit, it is a pittance.'

'Must be some ranch!'

'Bridger County is real good cattle country an' so, if'n' this ranch is its biggest an' best, wa'al. . . .'

'I git the picture.'

At this juncture, Red Ned Davis suddenly slammed his fist down on the table, causing all the whiskey glasses to jump.

'I got me a better idea!' he exclaimed.

'Yeah?'

'Yeah, Hank. An' it don't involve us killin' this Abe Fletcher feller.'

'It don't?'

'No. We git him to give us the three thousand.'

This time it was Vic Morgan's turn to laugh.

'Why, in blue blazes, would he do that?' he rasped.

'Because, in exchange, we'd make certain he kept his rightful inheritance,' replied the red-headed outlaw.

'An' jest how would we do that?' demanded Morgan.

'All we gotta do is kill his father 'fore he changes his will.'

'You're sure awful goddam keen to kill *somebody*,' commented the homesteader. Nevertheless, he considered this new proposal for a little while and finally nodded his head and remarked, 'You know, that's mebbe not such a bad idea.'

'You're darned tootin' it ain't!' chortled Davis.

'It's one helluva good idea,' declared Jolley eagerly. 'If'n' Abe Fletcher really reckons three thousand dollars to be nuthin' in comparison to this here ranch, then I guess he'll be only too willin' to pay that sum for us to make certain he gits his inheritance.'

'He will undoubtedly agree to our proposal,' said Davis. 'There's no question of that.'

'But, once we've secured him his inheritance, he could easily renege on the deal,' said Jolley.

'Hmm, that's a good point,' admitted Davis.

'I don't think so,' said Morgan.

'No?' said his cousin.

'No, Hank. You an' Ned have one helluva reputation. You're both wanted for armed robbery an' murder. Abe Fletcher ain't no fool. He'll know that, if'n' he fails to pay up, you'll come lookin' for him. An' he sure won't wanna be the richest *an' deadest* rancher in Bridger County!'

The two desperadoes laughed harshly.

' 'Course. He won't dare renege,' agreed Jolley.

'So, we go with your plan, Ned,' said Morgan.

'Yeah. S'posin' this here Abe Fletcher agrees,' said Jolley.

'An' s'posin' he don't?' growled Davis.

'Then, we think again,' replied the homesteader. 'But I don't reckon we'll need to. If he wants to hold on to that ranch, then he will accept our offer, I feel certain.'

'He may quibble, try to beat us down, pay us less than the full three thousand.'

'Mebbe, Ned, though I doubt it,' said Morgan. 'Anyways, should he try, I'll simply tell him that it's three thousand or no deal.'

'OK, Vic, let's go ahead.' Hank Jolley picked up the whiskey bottle and re-filled the three glasses. Then he raised his glass in a short, succinct toast: 'To our success!'

'To our success!' echoed the other two, whereupon all three lifted the glasses to their lips.

When they had drunk the toast, Red Ned Davis eyed the homesteader closely and said, 'Before you go an' broach Mr Fletcher, we'd best agree how we're gonna split the three thousand between us.'

'One thousand apiece,' replied Morgan.

'It's me an' your cousin who'll be doin' the killin'. We'll be takin' all the risks,' Davis pointed out.

'So?'

'So, I figure me an' Hank deserve the lion's share.'

'Oh, no! It was me who told you two 'bout Abe Fletcher an' his "pittance" in the first place.'

'An' me who came up with a plan to persuade him to part with it.'

'But. . . .'

'Hold on, the pair of you!' rasped Hank Jolley. 'We ain't even got the loot, yet here we are arguin' 'bout how to split it between us.'

'What are you sayin'?' enquired Morgan.

'I'm sayin' one thousand dollars is a heap more'n I've ever succeeded in holdin' in my life. So, I'm with you, cousin. I'll be quite satisfied if we each git one thousand.' Jolley turned to his fellow outlaw and added, 'Don't forget, Ned, that Vic is the go-between. When the job's done, we gotta rely on him to hand over our shares.'

'That's right,' averred Morgan. 'When the news of his father's death comes through, I'm gonna be the one who's there in town alongside Abe.'

'An' you'll grab the money an' bring it straight out here?' demanded Davis.

'If this is where you wanna rendezvous?'

'I think so, Vic. The search for us will have moved on by then. But we can settle that li'l matter after you've spoken to Fletcher,' said Jolley.

'Sure we can,' agreed Morgan. 'However, 'fore I go an' broach Abe with our plan, I want it agreed we each take an equal share of the money.'

'Agreed,' said his cousin promptly.

'Agreed,' said Red Ned Davis, though with some degree of reluctance.

Vic Morgan smiled. He lifted his whiskey glass and proceeded to drain it. The others followed suit. Thereupon, Morgan picked up the bottle and splashed some more whiskey into his guest's glasses. But, before he could refill his own, Davis grasped hold of his wrist.

'Sorry, Vic,' he said. 'You gotta be sober when you speak to this Fletcher feller.'

'I am sober!' protested Morgan.

'An' I intend that you stay that way,' said Davis, wresting the bottle from the homesteader's hand.

'Aw, c'mon!'

'No, Vic. Ned's right. You gotta have a clear head,' said Jolley.

Morgan scowled, but made no attempt to re-claim the whiskey bottle. He had had two large whiskeys on top of the whiskey and beer he had consumed at the Silver Dollar. Consequently, he realized that another drink might prove one too many. He wasn't about to admit as much to the others, yet he decided not to force the issue. Instead, he rose to his feet.

'OK,' he said. 'I'll head back into town an' go speak to Abe Fletcher.'

'Good luck!' said Hank Jolley.

'Thanks.'

The homesteader left his companions drinking his whiskey and set off towards the town. He wondered whether Fletcher had finished the meal he had proposed to consume at the Alhambra and, if so, whether he had returned to the Silver Dollar or remained in the hotel. There was only one way to find out.

Morgan determined to try the saloon first. He entered through the batwing doors and ran his eye over the crowd in the bar-room. It was sparser than it had been immediately after the posse left town. And of Abe Fletcher there was no sign. Morgan turned on his heel and, on stepping outside, approached the saloonkeeper, George Young, who was standing on the sidewalk, idly watching the hustle and bustle of Calico City's Main Street and smoking a large Havana cigar.

George Young was a big man, immaculately clad in a black three-piece suit, white linen shirt, black bootlace tie, black Derby hat and highly-polished black leather shoes. He smiled inwardly. The Silver Dollar was enjoying very good business. He felt a little guilty at having replaced Arizona Audrey with a group of new young singers and dancers, yet he knew it was the right thing to do. And George Young was nothing if not pragmatic.

He was about to re-enter the saloon when Vic Morgan approached him.

'Afternoon, Mr Young,' said the homesteader.

'Afternoon, Mr Morgan,' replied Young.

'I . . . er . . . I was lookin' for somebody,' confided Morgan.

'Oh, yeah?'

'Yes. A newcomer to Calico City. We had us a few beers together earlier. But I don't see him there now.'

'A tall, good-lookin' feller in a Prince Albert coat?'

'Yeah – that's him. He went across to the Alhambra 'bout an hour or so back.'

'Then, I guess he's still there.'

'He hasn't returned to the Silver Dollar?'

'No, he ain't.'

'Thanks.'

Vic Morgan doffed his hat and the two men parted. George Young stepped back inside his saloon, while Morgan headed across Main Street towards the Alhambra Hotel.

# CHAPTER SEVEN

Morgan entered the lobby of the Alhambra and proceeded along it to the reception desk at its far end. He accosted the clerk standing behind the desk.

'Excuse me,' he said, 'but could you tell me whether Mr Abe Fletcher is at present in the hotel?'

'Yessir,' replied the clerk. 'He finished his lunch 'bout a quarter of an hour ago an' retired to his room.'

'An' which room would that be?'

The clerk indicated the stairs with a jerk of his thumb.

'Room Number Six,' he said. 'Head of the stairs, turn right.'

'Thanks.'

Morgan smiled and began to mount the stairs. He quickly found Room Number Six and knocked on the door with his knuckles. There was a slight delay before a voice from within enquired, 'Who is it?'

'Your acquaintance of this mornin', Vic Morgan. We had a coupla beers together at the . . .'

'. . . Silver Dollar.' Abe Fletcher completed his sentence for him and then promptly opened the door. 'Come in, Vic,' he said.

Morgan entered the room and, at Abe's invitation, sat down on the room's only chair. Abe, meanwhile, planted himself on the side of the bed.

'I know we'd arranged to meet at the saloon, but I've got somethin' I'm anxious to discuss with you,' explained Morgan.

'Oh, yeah?'

'Yes. I expect you've been thinkin' 'bout your pa disheritin' you?'

'I've thought of nuthin' else.'

'Wa'al, I've come up with a li'l scheme that jest might solve your problem.'

Abe's eyes brightened and he regarded the homesteader with sudden interest.

'In what way?' he asked eagerly.

'I've figured how we could prevent him.'

'You don't know my pa. He. . . .' began Abe.

'I don't need to,' Morgan interrupted him. 'Your pa won't be able to disinherit you if'n' he's dead, will he?' he asked.

'Er . . . no, he won't. But Pa ain't dead.'

'Not yet, he ain't.'

'Are you proposin' that I. . . ?'

'No. You won't be involved in your pa's death. I have arranged. . . .'

Abe suddenly leapt off the bed and put a finger to his lips.

'No more,' he said.

'What? I was jest gonna explain. . . .'

'Not here.' Abe looked around him and said quietly, 'Walls have ears.'

Morgan glanced at the walls between Abe Fletcher's room and those on either side of it and nodded.

'You're right,' he said. 'Let's discuss the matter elsewhere.'

'Over a few more beers at the Silver Dollar,' suggested Abe. 'It's still only early afternoon, so there won't be too many customers. We'll find us a table out of earshot of any that are there; mebbe sit at that corner table we occupied this mornin'?'

'Suits me.'

'Fine.' Abe strapped on his holster carrying his recently-purchased Colt Peacemaker and slapped his Stetson on his head. ''Let's go,' he said.

They quickly vacated the room and hurried off downstairs.

Behind them both Abe Fletcher's room and Room Number Five stood empty. However, Room Number Seven did not. Following a very satisfactory lunch in the hotel restaurant, Audrey had retired to her room, intending to rest there until Jack Stone returned. She assumed that the posse would head back to town once darkness began to fall, for there would be little point in continuing their search for the two fugitives in the dark. Although, she reflected hopefully, the posse might already have caught them and be on their way home.

As this thought crossed her mind, Audrey heard Vic Morgan knock on Abe Fletcher's door. The Alhambra's interior walls were almost paper-thin and, therefore, the blonde was able to listen to Abe's response and, once Morgan had been admitted to Room Number Six, the pair's subsequent conversation. She did not like what she heard.

When the two conspirators left the room and clattered off downstairs, Audrey immediately leapt up from the bed and hurried over to the window. From there she observed the pair cross Main Street and vanish through the batwing doors into the Silver Dollar Saloon.

What should she do? She was still in a state of shock, for, despite leading a pretty adventurous life, Audrey had never before overheard what she took to be a murder plot. If only Jack Stone hadn't left with the posse! And not only Stone. Audrey recalled that she had watched Marshal Dave Grant and his two deputies ride off. Calico City's entire complement of peace officers had abandoned the town.

Audrey fetched a chair across to the window and sat down. Since there was nobody to whom she could report, she determined to remain at the window and watch events. She intended to focus on the Silver Dollar and, should one or other of the two re-appear, then decide what to do next.

As she sat there, Audrey reflected that she knew the identity of one of the two men, namely Vic Morgan, a homesteader who lived just outside town and was a habitual frequenter of the Silver Dollar. As for the other, he was the man whom she and Stone had encountered that morning in the corridor outside their respective rooms. It would not be too difficult, she reckoned, to obtain his name, since he was sure to have signed the hotel register.

While Audrey kept watch on the saloon, Vic Morgan and Abe Fletcher crossed the bar-room and ordered a couple of beers. Morgan paid and then the pair headed for the same corner table that they had occupied earlier in the day. There were few customers in the bar-room and most of them were grouped round the bar. There was none within earshot of the corner table.

Abe raised his glass.

'Your good health!' he pronounced.

'An' yours,' replied the homesteader.

They each enjoyed a satisfying swig of beer and then Abe said quietly, 'So, what have you got in mind, Vic?'

'I got me a coupla fellers who would be willin' to eliminate your pa for a consideration.'

'What two fellers? Who are they?' demanded Abe.

The other smiled and shook his head. He had no intention of telling Abe that he was giving refuge to two wanted men. Nor was he about to inform him that one of the two outlaws was his cousin.

'That's somethin' you don't need to know,' he remarked. 'All I'll say is, that both are pretty goddam fast with a gun an' your pa won't be the first man they've shot.'

Abe nodded. He reckoned he knew who Vic Morgan's 'coupla fellers' were. He had listened to Marshal Dave Grant's appeal for volunteers and thought it was surely too much of a coincidence that the two bank robbers were in the vicinity at exactly the same time as Morgan's pair of gunslingers.

'Red Ned Davis an' Hank Jolley,' he said, grinning.

Morgan choked on his beer.

Then, when he had stopped spluttering, he rasped, 'What are you talkin' about?'

'I'm guessin' that the two fellers, who you say would be willin' to gun down my pa, are the same pair as the marshal an' his posse are lookin' for.'

'Yeah, but that's all it is, a guess.'

'Aw, c'mon, Vic! If'n we're gonna act together in this matter, then we must trust each other.'

'I s'pose.'

'I don't know how or why Red Ned Davis an' Hank Jolley chose to hide out at your homestead, an' I don't care. But you gotta level with me.'

Vic Morgan grunted and took another swig of his beer. He had to admit there was merit in what Abe Fletcher said. Murder was a serious business and those engaged in it had to rely on each other. Completely. He smiled wryly and shrugged his shoulders.

'OK,' he said. 'I admit it. You guessed correctly.'

'That's better.'

'They're jest passin' through. Needed to rest their hosses, that's all.'

'An' you say they would be happy to kill Pa for a consideration. How much?'

'Those three thousand dollars which he gave you as a pay-off.'

'That's one helluva lotta money.'

'A mere pittance, you called it.'

'Everythin's relative. You wouldn't see it as such, nor, it seems, would your pals.'

'No.'

'So, mebbe we can negotiate a reasonable price.'

'No.'

'No?'

'No, Abe.' Vic Morgan smiled slyly. 'This ain't open for negotiation. You pay us the three thousand and we ensure you inherit the ranch – the biggest an' the best in the whole of Bridger County, you said.'

'Wa'al. . . .'

'Otherwise there's no deal.'

Abe Fletcher frowned. He felt that Morgan's demand was exorbitant, yet he was desperate to inherit. With his pa dead, he would be Bridger County's wealthiest citizen. Indeed, he would probably be the richest man in the whole state of Wyoming.

So, he would not be particularly popular with some of Snake Springs' townsfolk. His father had said they might get together and string him up. Well, let them try. He wasn't afraid of a few townies. And, anyway, Snake Springs would need his business more than he needed Snake Springs. In fact, he could easily avoid the town altogether. There were several other towns situated not too far from the Triple F ranch which he could patronise instead. His frown vanished as he visualised himself the uncrowned king of Bridger County.

'OK, it's a deal,' he said decisively.

'Good! Let's shake on it,' said Vic Morgan.

The two men shook hands.

'We ain't got much time in which to act,' remarked Abe. 'Like I told you, Pa said he would be makin' out his new will tomorrow mornin' when he an' Brett ride into town to fetch supplies.'

'He ain't likely to change his mind 'bout that?'

'No, Vic. Pa collects supplies every Friday reg'lar as clockwork. Leaves the ranch at eight o' clock sharp. He ain't gonna change that routine. Not for nobody, nor nuthin'.' Abe Fletcher smiled and added, 'He can't, for that mornin' he also collects sufficient cash from the bank to pay the hands' wages.'

'Right. An' his decision to cut you outta his will. . . .'

'Is final. Pa ain't gonna alter his mind on that score. So, if'n' I'm to remain heir to the Triple F, he's gotta die 'fore he reaches town. I suggest, therefore, that Red Ned Davis an' Hank Jolley intercept him somewhere 'tween the ranch an' Snake Springs.'

'How far is Snake Springs from here?'

'You follow the main trail towards Pocatello, Idaho. Snake Springs is on it, 'bout fifty miles from Calico City. A fair ride.'

'If Ned an' Hank start out this evenin' once it's dusk, an' ride on through the night, they should easily reach Snake Springs 'fore eight o' clock.'

'I agree.'

'An' jest where is the ranch in relation to the town?'

'It's a coupla miles to the west of Snake Springs,' said Abe and he explained, 'Your pals won't need to ride through the town, for the main trail skirts it an' then proceeds on towards the state line. The Triple F is situated jest beyond a small stand of cottonwoods. From the cover of those trees you can see where the fork leadin' to the ranch leaves the trail. 'Deed, there's a sign there, bearin' the words, "Triple F Ranch". They can't miss it.'

'So, Ned an' Hank need only hide up in the cottonwoods an' then jump out an' intercept your pa an' your brother when they turn on to the trail.'

'Yup. Pa an' Brett, they'll be ridin' a buckboard.'

'They won't have no ranch-hands with 'em?'

'I don't imagine so. But if they do, wa'al, two hot-shot gunslingers oughta be capable of gunnin' down a few cowpokes.'

'I guess.'

'Good!'

'An' once we git news of the deaths of your pa an'

your brother, I expect you to hand over the three thousand dollars.'

'Of course. That was the deal.' Abe suddenly frowned. 'Unless Pa or Brett has told someone I was headed for Calico City, nobody will know I'm here,' he mused.

'So?'

'So, I can't go an' claim my inheritance until I git that news. We're in a different county an' fifty-odd miles from Snake Springs. S'pose the news don't spread this far?'

'It's sure to. Eventually. You'll jest need to stay put till it does.'

'An' you an' your pals will need to wait for the three thousand. You can't expect me to pay out simply on your pals' say-so.'

'No.' This time it was Vic Morgan who frowned. He had no wish that his cousin and Red Ned Davis should hang around his homestead for any longer than was strictly necessary. He had planned that they should return from Bridger County, collect their share of the blood money and promptly depart. 'I agree that news of your pa's death has to come from someone other than Hank or Ned. But how. . . ?'

'I've got it!' declared Abe, as inspiration suddenly struck him. 'I'll wire Pa.'

'Whaddya mean?' gasped a puzzled Vic Morgan.

'Tomorrow I shall send him a telegraph along the lines of:

*I have taken your advice and intend starting up a horse ranch. I aim to do so in Sun Valley, Idaho. I shall need to pass through Bridger County. I should like, therefore, to stop off and see the old homestead for one last time. Will you allow this? Please reply to me at the Alhambra Hotel, Calico City. Abe.*

'Wa'al, d'you think that'll do the trick? It's certain to elicit some kinda response from my soon-to-be widowed sister-in-law. She's bound to give me the sad news of Pa's an' Brett's deaths.'

A wide smile split Morgan's thin, weather-beaten features.

'Yeah,' he said. 'That li'l ploy oughta work.'

'An' soon as I git the reply to my wire, I'll pay out an' then head west an' claim my inheritance. The Triple F will be mine,' stated Abe, cheerfully reflecting that there would now be no change of name to Double F.

'I reckon you're as good as there,' said Morgan.

Smiling, Abe agreed, and he added, 'So, let me buy us a coupla drinks an' then you can return to your homestead an' tell your pals what's been agreed between us.'

'I sure will. An' I'll return later jest to let you know Hank an' Ned are on their way.'

'Thanks. I'll be at the hotel since, until I know for sure that Pa an' Brett are dead, I don't figure on doin' no more drinkin'. The time to celebrate will be when the deed is done.'

'Right.'

Abe this time fetched a couple of large whiskeys. Both men raised their glasses in a silent toast before throwing back the amber liquid in one gulp. Then they shook hands and headed across the saloon towards the batwing doors, the homesteader a few paces ahead of Abe Fletcher.

As Abe stepped between the batwing doors, he chanced to glance across the street and observe Audrey sitting at her bedroom window. He noted that she seemed to be focusing her gaze on the Silver Dollar and hastily stepped backwards. Then, from just inside the saloon, he watched Audrey disappear from view and, a few moments later, emerge from the Alhambra's front door and set off in the wake of the departing homesteader. Abe pushed open the batwing doors and proceeded to follow the blonde.

He recalled his conversation with Vic Morgan when the latter had first broached the idea of eliminating his father. Had the blonde been in the next-door bedroom at the time and, if so, had she overheard their conversation? The fact that she was heading off down Main Street after Morgan suggested that she had. Abe increased his pace.

Audrey, meantime, had crossed the street and was hurrying along the sidewalk some distance behind her quarry. What, she asked herself, was she proposing to do? She didn't rightly know, yet, in the absence of Jack Stone, the marshal and the posse, she felt she had to do something. If nothing else, she could mount a vigil on Morgan's homestead and perhaps observe him make his next move. Since arriving in Calico City in July, Audrey had struck up a friendship with Diamond Lil, a voluptuous redhead who ran a very successful bordello on the edge of town. From the bordello's front parlour window one could see quite clearly Vic Morgan's ramshackle dwelling. It was from here that Audrey proposed to keep watch.

She was not, however, destined to enter the bordello. Before reaching it, she was overtaken by Abe Fletcher. He crept up behind her and rammed his Colt Peacemaker into the small of her back.

'Keep walkin' an' say nuthin',' he snarled.

'But. . . .'

'Shuddup!'

Audrey felt the colour drain from her cheeks. If only she had stayed put at the hotel until Stone's return, she thought bitterly. She glanced at her companion. He was, she noted, the man who occupied Room Number Six! It was not surprising, therefore, that Audrey should be in fear of her life.

While Audrey was setting off after Vic Morgan and Abe was setting off after her, their movements were being observed by a third party, namely George Young. The big saloonkeeper liked to keep a watchful eye on everything that happened within the bounds of the Silver Dollar. Earlier, he had noticed Vic Morgan enter with a stranger and the pair conduct in low tones an earnest conversation, at the conclusion of which they raised glasses in some form of toast. Intrigued, Young had watched them leave the saloon and, upon stepping outside, he had stood and marked their progress, and that of Audrey, along Main Street in the direction of Morgan's homestead. That the blonde was tracking Morgan and the stranger tracking Audrey, George Young had little doubt. He did not, however, see Abe prod Audrey with his revolver, for they were some distance away and Abe's body shielded the gun from Young's sight. He watched until all three had vanished inside Morgan's dwelling. Then, although still intrigued, the saloonkeeper turned and went back inside the Silver Dollar.

Meantime, Vic Morgan had barely begun to tell his cousin and Red Ned Davis of his conversation with Abe Fletcher when the latter pushed open the door to Morgan's dwelling and bundled Audrey inside.

'This li'l lady's been eavesdroppin'. Her hotel bedroom's next to mine,' he said gruffly.

'No .. .no, I . . . I ain't! I ain't heard nuthin'!' protested the blonde, blanching as she recognized Red Ned Davis from a Wanted poster she had seen pinned up outside the law office.

'Shuddup!' Abe faced Morgan and the two outlaws. He had not replaced the Colt Peacemaker in his holster and he had no intention of doing so until he was safely out of Morgan's homestead and well on his way up Main Street towards his hotel. With the three thousand dollars still in the canvas bag inside

111

his coat pocket, he felt pretty darned vulnerable. 'I'll leave it to you boys to deal with the lady an' then do what you gotta do to earn the sum we agreed on. OK, Vic?' he said.

'OK, Abe.'

'Fine.'

Abe turned on his heel and left the dwelling, slamming the door shut behind him. Morgan crossed the room and grabbed hold of Audrey. Then he half-turned and watched through the window as Abe hurried off down the path, past several rows of potatoes, flaxseed and beans, to where it connected with the main trail into town.

When Abe had disappeared into Main Street, Morgan dragged Audrey over to the kitchen table and plonked her down on one of the chairs.

'Now,' he snarled. 'Spill the beans. Jest how much did you hear back at the hotel?'

'I . . . I told you. I heard nuthin'.'

'Liar!'

'No. I . . . I. . . .'

'Vic's right – you're lyin',' rasped Red Ned Davis, his bearded countenance grim and his grey eyes as hard as granite.

'No . . . no, I ain't, I swear!' cried Audrey.

'You can swear all you like, but none of us believes you,' said Hank Jolley.

'Yeah. So, jest button your lips,' snapped Morgan. He glanced at his cousin. 'What are we gonna do with her?' he asked nervously.

112

'We ain't got no choice. We gotta kill her,' stated Davis.

'No!' cried Audrey, struggling to her feet and screaming for help.

However, her screams were quickly cut short as Davis clamped a large, rough hand over her mouth.

'Git some cord an' somethin' to gag her with,' he directed Vic Morgan.

'Yeah, do that, cousin, an' be quick about it,' added Jolley curtly.

Morgan hurried to do as he was bid and, a few moments later, Audrey found herself bound to the kitchen chair with a length of whipcord and gagged with one of Morgan's kerchiefs.

'Now we can discuss what's to be done without her screamin' her head off,' muttered the homesteader.

'There ain't nuthin' to discuss,' retorted Davis. 'We kill her.'

'An' then what?'

'We bury her here. There's plenty of space outside on your smallholdin',' said Jolley.

'Oh, no! You ain't buryin' her here!' protested Morgan.

'Why not?'

'Because, cousin, I ain't plannin' on stickin' around once I git my share of those three thousand dollars.'

'So?'

'So, whoever rents this land after me might easily dig up her corpse. An' then I'd be a wanted man.'

113

'But you'd be gone from here. How'd they find you, eh?'

'Even so. An', anyways, what if someone comes lookin' for her before I depart, an' spots a patch of recently dug soil 'bout the right size for a grave?'

'Why would anyone? Who is she, anyway?'

'A saloon singer by the name of Arizona Audrey. She's jest recently been sacked by the proprietor of the Silver Dollar.'

'There you are, then! Nobody's gonna come lookin'. Folks will jest assume she's left town,' remarked Davis.

'Mebbe . . . Mebbe not.' Morgan scratched his jaw thoughtfully. 'It ain't a chance I'm willin' to take. Why don't you take her with you tonight when you head off for Bridger County. You can drop off her body somewhere 'tween here an' there.'

'We go tonight?' said Davis.

'Yeah.' Morgan smiled and went on to tell the two outlaws what Abe Fletcher had told him about his father heading into Snake Springs on the following morning to collect supplies and, at the same time, change his will. He explained Abe's plan for the ambush. 'So, there you are. If'n' you set out once it's dusk, you should easily reach them cottonwoods 'fore Mr Fletcher an' his younger son leave the Triple F.'

'Will do,' said Davis. 'But we ain't takin' the woman with us. No, sirree! Let's jest concentrate on earnin' them three thousand dollars.'

'So, what are we gonna do 'bout Arizona Audrey?' exclaimed Morgan.

'D'you git many visitors?'

'Nope. Can't remember the last time anyone called.'

'Good! In that case, you keep her a prisoner till we git back. Then, when your pal, Abe Fletcher, pays up, me an' Hank'll hit the trail an' take the woman with us. We'll shoot her an' dump her body somewhere out in the mountains of the Wind River Range.'

Relieved, Vic Morgan smiled.

'That's a deal,' he said.

Thereupon, they settled down to wait for darkness to fall.

# CHAPTER EIGHT

The light was fading fast when Marshal Dave Grant and his posse turned about and headed back towards Calico City. They had searched several gulches and ravines around the foothills that lay between the town and the Wind River Range. Indeed, they had gone round in circles, endeavouring to cover all possible hiding-places within the county's bounds. But to no avail. They had seen neither hair nor hide of the two fugitives and, with darkness beginning to fall, Grant had finally cried a halt to their search.

Now, though disappointed, they spurred on their horses as they made for home. Weary, thirsty and hungry, all were anxious to reach the town and find rest and sustenance. Even Jack Stone, who had more reason than any of them to want to hunt down the bandits, accepted that there was no point in continuing the chase any longer. He would have to wait until the following day to resume his pursuit of Red Ned Davis. Perhaps by then the marshal might have received news by telegraph of a sighting of the pair. As it was, Stone had no idea as to which direction they had taken.

Upon reaching the town, the posse split up and went their several ways. The marshal and his two deputies dismounted immediately outside the law office, while Jack Stone climbed out of the saddle and hitched his bay gelding to the rail in front of the Alhambra Hotel.

He entered and made his way along the lobby towards the stairs. He greeted the clerk at the reception desk and asked for his key.

'I guess you didn't catch them two murderin' varmints,' said the clerk.

'No. 'Fraid not,' replied Stone. 'Anyways, jest gimme the key.'

'I ain't got it. Arizona Audrey still has it. She took it with her.'

'You mean she ain't in our room?'

'That's right. She went out sometime after the posse left town an' she ain't returned.'

'D'you know where she went?'

The clerk shook his head.

'Nope,' he said. 'She came downstairs in one heck of a hurry an' shot off out.'

'I take it she didn't have her luggage with her when she left?' said Stone.

'Oh, no, sir! If she had, I wouldn't have let her leave without payin'. Mebbe she's gone visitin' or shoppin'?'

'Yeah. Mebbe? But why was she in such a hurry?'

'I couldn't say.'

'OK. Wa'al, thanks.'

Stone had expected to find the blonde somewhere in the hotel, either in her room or in the restaurant or bar-room. Where could she be? Stone retraced his steps along the lobby and walked outside. He peered up and down Main Street. Who did she know in Calico City that she would be likely to visit? He had no idea, but he knew a man who might.

Stone crossed the street and entered the Silver Dollar. It was pretty full, for most of the posse had dropped in for a beer. He accosted one of them.

'Can you point out Mr George Young to me?' he asked.

'Yeah. That's him over there, the big feller talkin' to the mayor,' the man replied, pointing to where the saloonkeeper stood near the bar, conversing with the fat mayor and two or three other of the town's dignitaries.

Stone stepped across to the bar and ordered a beer. Then he waited until there was a lull in the conversation and, immediately there was, he addressed the saloonkeeper.

'Mr George Young?'

'Yeah, who's askin'?'

The saloonkeeper turned round and faced the Kentuckian.

'That's the famous Jack Stone,' the mayor informed him.

Young smiled broadly as he observed the gun-fighter.

'Yeah, I was standin' there when you volunteered to join the posse,' he said and, extending his hand, he remarked, 'Pleased to meet you, Mr Stone. What can I do for you?'

They shook hands and Stone replied, 'I'm lookin' for your one-time saloon singer, Arizona Audrey. She was stayin' with me at the Alhambra, but she ain't there now an' I was wonderin' if you could suggest where she might be? Has she any partickler friend in town she may be visitin'?'

'She has: Diamond Lil; she runs a bordello on the edge of town.'

'Thanks. If you could point me in the right direction. . . .'

'I don't think she's with Lil.'

'Oh?'

'Let me explain. I'm an observant kinda feller. When you run a saloon, you need to be. You wanna know what's what.'

'So?'

'Earlier today, jest after you an' the posse left town, I was in the saloon when I noticed one of my regular customers, a homesteader named Vic Morgan, deep in conversation with a stranger – a tall, good-lookin' feller in a Prince Albert coat. After a li'l while, they parted. But then, sometime later, Vic Morgan returned to town. I was standin' outside the saloon takin' the air an' I watched him stroll from the direction of his homestead an' enter the saloon. However, he didn't stay in there above a few minutes.'

'No?'

'No. He came out an' asked me if'n' I'd seen the feller he'd been talkin' to an' had he returned to the Silver Dollar? When I informed him that he hadn't, Morgan thanked me an' entered the Alhambra, while I headed back into the saloon. A few minutes passed and then Morgan an' the stranger also entered the saloon. They sat at a corner table well away from any of my other customers an' kept their voices low. I surmised they was plottin' somethin', which kinda roused my curiosity.'

'Go on,' said Stone, intrigued.

'Wa'al, eventually, they left again. I followed, but discreetly, an' neither of 'em spotted me. Morgan left first. The stranger was about to follow him outside when he happened to glance towards the upper floor of the Alhambra. I followed his gaze an' saw Arizona Audrey at her bedroom window, starin' down at Morgan. Then she vanished. Moments later, I saw her head off along Main Street in the same direction as that taken by Vic Morgan. An' once she'd passed by the saloon, the stranger stepped outside an' followed her.' Young smiled and added, 'At that point, I, too, stepped outside. I watched all three proceed down Main Street an' noticed the stranger catch up with Arizona. All of 'em crossed the town limits an' turned off the trail on to Vic Morgan's run-down homesteadin'. It's situated on the left, 'bout a quarter of a mile east of the town. I couldn't see from where I was standin', but I assume they all entered his dwellin'.'

'Hmm.'

'Which is why I don't think Arizona is at Diamond Lil's bordello. 'Course, it's possible that later she left Vic Morgan's homestead an' *did* visit her friend. Lil's bordello is the last building' on the right as you leave town, goin' east.'

'This was sometime back when Audrey an' the others went to Morgan's homestead?'

'Oh, yeah! Coupla hours or more – mebbe three. All that to-in' an' fro-in' took up quite some time.'

'Thank you, Mr Young.'

'Not at all. Hope you find her, Mr Stone.'

'So do I.'

Stone set off along the street towards the homestead. A worried frown creased his brow. Although he had no idea why Audrey should have chosen to follow the homesteader, or the stranger to follow her, his instincts told him that something was wrong and that she had put herself in danger.

Since he had to pass the bordello on his way to the homestead, Stone called in. After all, he thought, perhaps Audrey had made two visits that afternoon and was even now sitting chatting to her friend, Diamond Lil? However, he was disappointed. When he called and asked if Arizona Audrey was inside, the redhead shook her head.

'No,' said Lil. 'Arizona ain't called today.'

'Mebbe you saw her go by?' Stone indicated Vic Morgan's homestead with a jerk of his thumb. 'Thataway?'

Lil shook her head. 'No.'

'OK. Thanks.'

'Is there somethin' the matter? Is Arizona in some kinda trouble?'

'I dunno. But I aim to find out.'

Stone turned and left the bordello. Behind him, the red-headed proprietress looked distinctly worried.

'Let me know what's what,' she called after him.

'Will do,' he replied and continued on his way.

By now dusk was fading into night. Stone proceeded slowly along the trail to the boundary of Vic Morgan's run-down property. He could see a light shining in the window of the homesteader's dwelling. He turned off the trail and began to walk silently up the path towards the house. His years as an Army scout trained by a Kiowa brave enabled him to glide noiselessly over the rough dirt surface of the path and then, just as he reached the house, he heard the sound of horses' hoofs receding away from its rear. He hurried round to the back of the building and was in time to glimpse two shadowy figures on horseback vanish into the darkness.

Stone paused and then re-traced his steps. There was a small side-window. He crept up to it and cautiously peered inside. The sight of Audrey sitting bound and gagged at the kitchen table shook him.

His instincts had evidently not played him false. He directed his gaze at the other figure seated at the table. Vic Morgan sat opposite the blonde, staring malevolently at her and, at the same time, drinking whiskey straight from the bottle. The bottle, Stone noted, was half-empty.

The Kentuckian crept back the way he had come until he reached the front door. Thereupon, he drew his Frontier Model Colt from its holster and, in one swift movement, threw open the door and leapt into the room. The sound of the door crashing back against the wall caused Vic Morgan to drop the whiskey bottle and swirl round in his chair. He staggered to his feet and headed across the room to the far wall, where his ancient shotgun hung.

'I wouldn't, if I was you!' shouted Stone.

Morgan raised his hand towards the gun, then changed his mind and reluctantly lowered it. He turned to face the intruder.

'Who . . . who in blue blazes are you? An' why. . . ?'

'I'll ask the questions,' rasped Stone. 'You jest shuddup an' stay exactly where you are. Make a move towards that shotgun an' I'll blow your brains out.'

Morgan opened his mouth to reply, but thought better of it and remained stock-still, his face drained of all colour, his eyes fearful and fixed upon the Kentuckian.

Stone placed the revolver on the kitchen table. He reckoned he would surely reach it long before Morgan could turn and grab hold of his shotgun.

Morgan seemingly reckoned likewise, for he made no effort to reach for the weapon. He merely stood and watched while Stone released Audrey from her gag and the whipcord which bound her.

'Gee, thanks, Jack!' she gasped. 'I . . . I thought I was done for.'

She rose and stood beside the Kentuckian, who picked up the Frontier Model Colt and aimed it once more at the transfixed homesteader.

'Now,' said Stone, 'tell me what in tarnation's goin' on?'

'It all began jest after you left town with the posse,' replied Audrey, and she went on to tell the Kentuckian about the snatch of conversation she had overheard in her hotel room.

'This roused my suspicions. They was obviously plannin' a murder,' she explained.

'So, what did you do next?' he asked.

'Since you an' the marshal an' his deppities had all left town, I reckoned all I could do was to try to keep an eye on things. Which I did.' She thereupon informed Stone of the vigil she had kept at her bedroom window and of how she had decided to follow Vic Morgan when he left the Silver Dollar Saloon. 'Unfortunately, I was spotted by his fellow conspirator who rammed a gun in my back an' brought me here, where I found them two outlaws the posse was lookin' for: Red Ned Davis an' Hank Jolley. I recognized Davis from a Wanted notice I'd seen stuck up outside the law office,' she concluded.

'So, what exactly is this murder plot that you over-heard back at the Alhambra? Are Red Ned Davis an' Hank Jolley involved in it?'

'Oh, yes! The feller in the hotel room next to ours is named Abe Fletcher an' he's heir to the Triple F ranch over in Bridger County. Only his father is plannin' to disinherit him. So, he's hired Davis an' Jolley to kill his father 'fore he can do so.'

'I see.' Stone stared Vic Morgan straight in the eye. 'You better tell me everythin' – an' I mean everythin' – unless you wanna swing,' he snarled.

'No! No, I can't! I daren't!' protested Morgan.

'We gotta prevent this killin'. If we do, you'll face a jail sentence. But, if we don't, you'll hang for certain as an accessory to murder.'

Morgan blanched and nervously felt his neck. He had no wish to betray his cousin and Red Ned Davis. On the other hand, he had even less wish to hang, and he feared that, unless he did betray his co-conspirators, he would in fact end up on the gibbet.

'OK,' he muttered. 'I'll . . . I'll tell you what our plans are.'

And he was as good as his word. He told Stone about his first conversation with Abe Fletcher and how, afterwards, he had found Hank Jolley and Red Ned Davis hiding out at the homestead. Then he described how they had decided to eliminate Abe's father and his brother in exchange for the three thousand dollars Abe had received from his father.

'That's kinda ironic, ain't it?' growled Stone.

'Fletcher's pa payin' for his own murder? Anyway, go on. I need to know how your cousin an' his pardner propose to commit this crime.'

'It's like this. . . .' And Morgan proceeded to describe in detail the plot to ambush Robert B. and Brett Fletcher and gun them down.

Stone turned to Audrey.

'Can you confirm any of this?' he asked.

'Oh, yes!' she replied eagerly. 'That's exactly as I heard it. They was discussin' it in front of me. Guess they figured it didn't matter what I heard, since they was proposin' to kill me on their return.'

'Right. In that case, we ain't got no time to lose. If'n' I'm gonna git to Bridger County in time to prevent these killin's, I'll need to set out straight-away.'

'What about Abe Fletcher? Ain't you gonna hand him over to the marshal?'

'Nope. He can wait. He won't be goin' anywhere. He'll jest be sittin' in the Alhambra waitin' news of his pa's death.' Stone paused, as a sudden thought struck him, and then he continued, 'We don't want him to suspect that everythin' ain't goin' accordin' to plan. So, we mustn't let him see me takin' this sono-fabitch to the law office, or see you either, for you're supposed to be a prisoner here.'

'That's OK,' said Audrey. 'I'll stay at Lil's bordello till everythin's settled. She'll be happy to put me up, I'm sure.'

'Fine. An' I'll take him by a back route, thereby

avoidin' Main Street,' said Stone, indicating an extremely crestfallen Vic Morgan.

Thereupon, they left the homestead and made their way back towards town. They parted outside Diamond Lil's bordello. Audrey slipped inside, while Stone took Morgan at gun-point round the rear of the bordello and then past the backs of all the houses and stores that lined Main Street between the bordello and the law office.

He rapped on the rear door of the law office and waited. Eventually, it was unlocked and opened by Deputy Marshal Walter Coburn.

The young deputy stared in surprise at the Kentuckian, who stood with his revolver rammed hard into the small of Vic Morgan's back.

'What in blue blazes. . . ?' he began.

'I need to speak to the marshal,' said Stone.

# CHAPTER NINE

When Stone, Morgan and Deputy Coburn, having passed the cells at the rear of the law office, stepped into the office itself, they found Marshal Dave Grant seated behind his desk and Deputy Nick O'Brien standing framed in the doorway. O'Brien had been about to begin his rounds of the town. However, he stopped and closed the door, reflecting that his rounds could wait until he found out what had brought Stone to the office.

Dave Grant glanced up, a quizzical look in his eye. He pushed aside the papers he had been examining.

'What's goin' on, Mr Stone?' he asked. 'Why are you holdin' that gun on Vic Morgan?'

'It's a long story, but I'll make it as brief as possible,' replied Stone.

'I'm listenin'.'

'OK. It's like this.'

Stone swiftly and succinctly explained what had brought him and Vic Morgan to the law office. When he had finished, the marshal whistled softly and said,

'We ain't got no time to lose.'

'We?'

'I figure you're goin' after them two bushwhackers?'

'I am.'

'Then, I'm comin' with you.'

'But you've got Calico City to look after, an' 'sides – Bridger County's outta your jurisdiction.'

'So what? I'm still ridin' with you, Mr Stone.' Marshal Grant turned to his two deputies. 'You boys can take care of the law round here while I'm gone, can't you?' he demanded.

'Sure can,' said Deputy O'Brien.

'You can rely on us,' added Deputy Coburn.

'I'm sure I can. OK, Walter, you place this varmint in one of our cells an' then stay here an' take care of the office. Nick, you carry on with your rounds.'

The two young deputies promptly did as they were bid, and Vic Morgan was taken away and confined to one of the law office's three cells. The other two, as it happened, lay empty.

Before Nick O'Brien departed, however, Stone instructed him and his compadre not to mention Vic Morgan's arrest to anyone.

'Nobody's to know he's in one of the cells – at least not until after me an' the marshal return. We don't want Abe Fletcher gittin' wind of what's happened,' he said. Then he asked Grant, 'D'you know the way to the Triple F? Do Abe Fletcher's instructions make sense?'

'Sure they do. I ain't familiar with the Triple F, but it should be easy enough to find where the fork to the ranch meets the trail. I can git us to Snake Springs and then we jest aim for them cottonwoods, where Hank Jolley an' Red Ned Davis are sure to be hangin' out.'

'As long as we git there 'fore they git to Mr Fletcher an' his son.'

'Yup. So, let's be on our way.'

The two stepped outside into Main Street and, as the door closed behind them, Walter Coburn returned from placing Vic Morgan in a cell. He smiled, went round behind the marshal's desk, and plonked himself down on to the marshal's chair.

Marshal Dave Grant untied his black mare from the hitching-rail outside the law office, while Stone crossed the street to the Alhambra Hotel and likewise released his bay gelding. Both men mounted and then, with the marshal leading, they cantered off up Main Street and out on to the trail, heading westwards in the direction of Bridger County.

It was a bright, starlit night and the trail was easy to follow. With a distance of some fifty miles to cover, they dared not break into a gallop. They did, however, proceed at a pretty fast canter. They needed to travel at the quickest possible speed their steeds could cope with if they were to reach their destination in time.

The minutes passed into hours and, eventually, the sky began to lighten. The sun slowly rose behind them in the east and, as they approached the out-skirts of Snake Springs, Dave Grant pulled his fob-watch from his vest pocket and glanced at the dial. The hands showed the time to be a quarter to eight.

'Jeez, we're cuttin' it fine!' he exclaimed, digging his heels into the mare's flanks and urging her on to greater speed.

Stone rode up beside him.

'How long have we got?' he shouted.

'Time enough, I reckon,' replied Grant. 'The trail skirts round the town, but, if we cut straight through, we'll save ourselves a good ten minutes.'

So saying, he took the fork that diverted from the main trail and went directly towards Snake Springs. The Kentuckian rode with him and both riders crossed the town limits and hurtled along a nearly deserted Main Street. Few townsfolk were about, though one or two storekeepers were in the process of opening up for business.

As they left Snake Springs and re-joined the trail, they passed a couple of buckboards on their way into town, driven by farmers on the same errand that was to bring Robert Fletcher and his son from the Triple F ranch. Grant and Stone continued to push their flagging mounts to the limit and then, all at once, they spotted a stand of cottonwoods, half a mile ahead.

'What time is it?' gasped Stone.

Grant again consulted his watch.

'Exactly eight o' clock,' he said.

'Accordin' to what Vic Morgan told us, that's the time Mr Fletcher an' his son are due to set out. Therefore, they'll be ridin' out on to this here trail pretty darned soon,' commented Stone.

'Yeah.'

Stone glanced to his left. A low hill bordered the trail on that side.

'Follow me,' he rasped.

He rode round behind the hill, followed by a rather puzzled Marshal Grant. Then, once they were out of sight of the trail, Stone turned the gelding's head and began to climb slowly up the rear side of the hill. Grant continued to follow him and, a few minutes later, both men cantered up on to the top of the hill. Beneath them were the cottonwoods, the trail and, a little to the west of the cottonwoods, a horse-track forking across grassland towards the distant Triple F ranch-house. Down this horse-track rattled a buckboard with two men up front. As it reached and turned left on to the trail, two horse-men suddenly rode out of the cottonwoods.

'Let's go!' cried Stone.

He and the marshal swooped down the hill, aiming to hit the trail half-way between the buck-board and the two outlaws who, concentrating their gaze on their intended victims, remained unaware of the others' approach until almost the last moment. Then, all at once, they turned to face the newcomers.

'Who in tarnation. . . ?' began Red Ned Davis,

pausing when he spotted Grant's badge of office pinned to his Prince Albert coat. Davis's mouth fell open and he cut short his question.

'Marshal Dave Grant,' said the lawman. 'An' you an' your confederate are under arrest,' he added, drawing his Colt Peacemaker from its holster.

'Like Hell we are!' snarled Davis.

He threw himself sideways out of the saddle, at the same time grabbing his revolver and, from beneath the horse, firing up at the marshal. His shot was hasty and, in consequence, missed. It whistled past Grant's left ear just as the marshal squeezed the trigger of his Colt Peacemaker. Grant did not miss. The slug struck Red Ned Davis plumb between the eyes and blasted his brains out.

Meantime, Hank Jolley and Jack Stone faced each other at a distance of about fifteen yards. Both men went for their guns. Stone was slower than of old, but he was still too quick and too accurate for the bank robber and would-be bushwhacker. The Frontier Model Colt barked twice. The first shot struck Jolley in the chest and the second hit him in the shoulder, toppling him out of the saddle.

Stone quickly dismounted and, gun in hand, strode across to where Jolley lay in the dust, a crimson patch spreading out from beneath his leather coat, as his life's blood oozed away. By the time Stone reached him, Jolley's eyes had glazed over and he was as dead as his companion, Red Ned Davis.

'That was pretty fast,' remarked Grant, as Stone

holstered his revolver.

'Not as fast as I used to be,' replied Stone, with a wry grin.

'No?'

'Nope. I'm thinkin' that mebbe it's 'bout time I gave up the gun. Anyways, between us, I reckon we did a good job. We did what we came here to do.'

'I should've let you take Davis, seein' as how it was your buddy he gunned down an' it was him, not Jolley, you was after,' said Grant.

Stone shook his head.

'It don't matter,' he retorted. 'Point is, both 'em no-account critters is dead, an' we've saved the state the cost of tryin' an' hangin' 'em.'

'Yeah. Guess so.'

'What in blue blazes is goin' on here?' a voice interrupted their conversation.

Stone and Grant transferred their gaze from the two bank robbers lying in the dust to Robert Fletcher, who had driven up in his buckboard and addressed them.

'Mr Fletcher?' enquired Grant.

'Robert B. Fletcher, an' this is my son, Brett,' replied the rancher, indicating the younger man beside him. 'But how'd you know who I was, for I sure as Hell don't know either of you two gents?' he added.

'Marshal Dave Grant. An' this here's Jack Stone, the famous Kentuckian gunfighter,' said Grant.

'Yeah. I've heard of you, Mr Stone. Who hasn't?

Anyways, who are those fellers you've jest shot?'

'A coupla the Brannigan gang. They recently attempted to rob the bank in Ellis Creek, but failed. These two are the only ones who escaped that botched raid. The rest were either shot dead or arrested,' said Grant.

'So, you tracked 'em here. But that still don't explain your knowin' who I am.'

'We didn't have to track Red Ned Davis an' Hank Jolley here. They weren't simply on the lam. They came here for a purpose.'

'Oh, yeah? An' what would that purpose be?'

'They was aimin' to kill you an' your son.'

'That's right,' interjected Stone. 'They was lyin' in wait in that thar stand of cottonwoods, waitin' for you to leave your ranch an' head into town as you invariably do each Friday mornin'.'

Robert Fletcher gasped in surprise.

'How . . . how'd they know 'bout that?' demanded an equally surprised Brett Fletcher.

'You've got an elder brother,' said Stone.

'Yeah.'

'He told 'em.'

Both father and son gazed open-mouthed in amazement at the Kentuckian.

Then presently, when he had recovered a little from his shock, the elder Fletcher said quietly, 'One of you'd best tell me the whole story.'

'Seems he was gonna pay those two galoots, an' an accomplice back in Calico City, who arranged

135

matters, three thousand dollars to gun you two down,' said the marshal.

The colour left the faces of both of the intended victims.

'Abe wanted us both dead?' exclaimed Robert B.

'An' he was prepared to use the money you gave him to achieve that end,' said Grant.

'Jeez!'

'Pa thought that givin' him that money was for the best. Abe could've used it to give hisself a fresh start well away from Bridger County,' said Brett.

'That was the plan,' confirmed his father.

'But he didn't,' said Stone.

'No.'

'He wasn't gonna give up his hopes of inheritin' the Triple F ranch.'

'No, Mr Stone, he wasn't. It's the finest spread in Bridger County; mebbe in all Wyoming. I guess he figured three thousand dollars was peanuts in comparison.'

'So, when he met a certain Vic Morgan an' Morgan proposed to arrange for your elimination 'fore you could change your will in favour of Brett, your elder son jumped at the idea.'

The rancher grimaced.

'You know 'bout his prison sentence an' how me an' Brett met him on his release?' he said.

Both Stone and the marshal nodded.

'I didn't want him back on the ranch. It was his conviction for murder that killed my dear wife.

136

'Sides, his return to Bridger County would've brought the whole matter up again. Folks had mostly forgotten it an' I wanted it to stay that way.'

'That's right. Although it was ten years ago that Abe killed poor old Willie Malone, he would've found there were some who had not forgotten an' regarded his sentence as too light. I believe there would have been big trouble if'n' he'd returned,' stated Brett.

'He was a fool not to have taken the money and moved on,' said Robert B. 'He could easily have made a decent new life for hisself with that to bank-roll him.'

'So, what happens now?' enquired Brett.

'We take these two bodies back into town an' notify the local marshal who they are. Then we head back to Calico City an' arrest your brother,' replied Grant.

'On what charge?' asked Robert B.

'On the charge of conspirin' to murder an', indeed, of instigatin' an' payin' for the said murder,' replied the marshal.

'Where will his trial take place?'

'In Calico City. That's where the plot was concocted an' where he's currently residin'.'

'So, news of it may not reach Bridger County?'

'No, it may not.'

'I jest hope it doesn't.'

'What are you proposin' to tell Marshal Jeff Huston?' demanded Brett.

'That's your local peace officer?' said Grant.

'Yeah.'

'I assume you would rather I didn't mention that these two were here in Bridger County on the behest of your elder son?' said Grant, as he pointed at the corpses.

'That's right, Marshal. There's surely no need for Huston or anybody else to know 'bout Abe's involvement?' replied the rancher.

'No, I guess not. I reckon we could simply say that, followin' the Ellis Creek bank raid, we was lookin' out for Red Ned Davis an' Hank Jolley. An' that we stumbled across their tracks an' trailed 'em to this spot, where we confronted an' shot 'em. What do you say, Mr Stone?'

'That's fine by me, Marshal,' replied the Kentuckian and, turning to the rancher, he said, 'We'll jest treat your arrival on the scene as coincidental.'

'Thanks.'

'D'you wanna load the two corpses on to the buckboard?' asked Brett.

'Yeah, that'd be handy,' replied Grant.

And so that was what they did. They lifted up the bodies of Red Ned Davis and Hank Jolley and dumped them on to the buckboard. Then they set off towards Snake Springs, with Robert Fletcher driving the buckboard and Jack Stone and Marshal Dave Grant leading the outlaws' two horses.

Upon reaching town, they proceeded along Main

138

Street as far as Jasper Bartlby's funeral parlour. Here they halted and, while Stone explained to the mortician what had happened and Bartlby and his assistant carried the corpses into the parlour, Grant continued along the street to the law office.

He entered and found Marshal Jeff Huston seated behind his desk, reading through some correspondence. Quickly, he told his counterpart about the shoot-out with the two bank robbers, while omitting any reference to their plot to way-lay and murder Robert Fletcher and his son.

'Wa'al, I'll be doggoned!' exclaimed Huston. 'So, that's the end of the Brannigan gang.'

'Yup,' said Grant. 'An' I don't reckon there'll be many folk who will mourn their passin'. Good riddance to the whole pack of 'em, I say.'

'I'll say amen to that,' responded Huston heartily, as he rose from his desk and headed for the door.

The two tall, similarly-clad marshals thereupon left the law office and set off towards the funeral parlour, outside of which a small crowd had gathered.

Once they arrived, they went inside, where they found Stone watching Jasper Bartlby and his assistant lay out the two corpses. Grant introduced Snake Springs' marshal to the Kentuckian.

'Pleased to meet you, Mr Stone,' said Huston, and the two men shook hands. Then he peered down at the dead outlaws. 'Yeah,' he said, 'I recognize the varmints from the "Wanted" posters I've got pinned up in my office. You an' Marshal Grant sure did well to rid us of those two no-account critters.'

'They did, didn't they?' said Robert Fletcher, who, together with his son, Brett, had just that moment entered the funeral parlour.

Huston turned to face the rancher.

'Howdy, Mr Fletcher,' he said. 'I noticed your buckboard outside.'

'Yeah. We brought the bodies into town. We was on our way here when we witnessed the confrontation between Mr Stone an' Marshal Grant an' the two deceased.'

'Of course. It's your day for comin' in an' pickin' up supplies, et cetera.'

'That's so.'

'Can I leave it to you, Marshal, to notify the law officers in an' around this territory that they no longer need go a-lookin' for Red Ned Davis an' Frank Jolley?' Grant asked his fellow peace officer.

'You certainly can,' replied Huston. 'I'll send wires to all the relevant law offices. An' I'll take care of the burials. I'll git our town council to pay for 'em to be interred in Boot Hill.'

'Thanks,' said Grant.

'I expect you'll be wantin' to git yourselves some breakfast an' then head back to Calico City?' remarked Huston.

'Wa'al, I figure our mounts will need restin' up 'fore we tackle the return journey,' said Grant.

'Yeah, an' I could do with restin' up myself,'

confessed Stone, adding, 'But you're right 'bout us wantin' some breakfast. I could eat a hoss. Whaddya say, Marshal?'

'Yup. Me, too,' grinned Grant.

'Ma Ferris's Eatin'-house serves a darned good breakfast,' said Huston. 'It's jest down the street. I'll show you the way.'

'Thanks,' said Grant.

'Me an' Brett, we'll soon finish our business. So, how's about, when you've eaten, you an' Mr Stone ride back to the ranch with us?' suggested Robert B.

'Wa'al. . . .'

'You can rest up there an' later, I'll show you round. An' I tell you, Brett's wife cooks the best T-bone steaks in the whole of Bridger County. Therefore, why don't you have supper with us an' stay the night? Then you can set out when you an' your hosses are real good an' rested.'

'That's mighty kind of you,' declared Grant.

'Sure is,' agreed Stone.

'So?'

The marshal and the Kentuckian exchanged glances.

'OK, I accept your offer,' said Grant finally, while Stone merely grinned and nodded his head.

Thereupon, leaving the mortician to his melancholy task, the five men left the funeral parlour. The two ranchers promptly parted from the others, driving their buckboard to the general store. Then, once they had purchased their supplies, they intended calling at their lawyer's office to change Robert Fletcher's will in favour of Brett. By the time all that had been taken care of, they expected that Jack Stone and Marshal Dave Grant would have finished downing a hearty breakfast at Ma Ferris's Eating-house.

In the meantime, the Kentuckian and Calico City's marshal had arrived at the eating-house and were enjoying mugs of hot, strong coffee while they waited for Ma Ferris to cook them their food. Jeff Huston had joined them for a coffee, though he intended returning to the law office when the breakfast eventually appeared. And, as they drank the coffee, all three happily discussed the morning's events and the desired demise of the notorious Red Ned Davis and Hank Jolley.

# CHAPTER TEN

It was shortly after dawn had risen on the following day, Saturday, when Jack Stone and Dave Grant sat down to breakfast with the Fletchers, both father and son. The meal was dished up by Brett's attractive young wife Sally and, like the supper the night before, was both delicious and plentiful.

As he was about to swallow a mouthful of egg and bacon, Stone commented, 'I'm sure gonna miss Sally's superb cookin' when we quit the Triple F an' head back to Calico City.'

'Wa'al, you'll be welcome to call back any time,' said Robert. 'Only next time you come, you'll see the signs have been changed. From now on, this here ranch is gonna be known as the Double F.'

'Severin' all links with your elder son?'

'That's right, Mr Stone.' Robert B frowned. 'I still can't git over the fact that Abe employed those two outlaws to kill me an' Brett.'

'Nor can I, Pa,' said Brett. 'How could he hate us

so much? Surely he realized that returnin' to Bridger County was not possible, that he needed to make a fresh start someplace else?'

'An' the three thousand dollars I gave him was more'n enough to help him make that fresh start,' declared Robert B.

'Yeah. It was very generous of you,' said Stone.

'He didn't seem to think so.'

'No.'

'Abe was always hot-headed an' liable to lose his temper, but to cold-bloodedly plot our murder. . . .' Brett left the sentence unfinished, before adding, 'I guess prison changed him.'

'Mebbe?' His father did not sound convinced. 'One thing's for sure. Abe wasn't about to accept that he'd lost his entitlement to the ranch. He wanted the Triple F real bad.'

'Yeah. Bad enough to kill for,' interjected Marshal Dave Grant.

'You said you're gonna arrest him, Marshal,' said Brett.

'I am.'

'If he's found guilty of conspiracy to murder, an' I'm sure he will be, what kinda sentence is he liable to git?'

'I am not sure, Brett. Could be a lengthy jail sentence. Could be he'll hang. It'll depend on the judge. There's one known as "String 'em up" Strachan. If your brother gits him presidin' at his trial, then he'll hang for certain.'

'I see.'

'Let's pray it doesn't come to that,' said Robert B. 'He's still my son an', despite what he's done or tried to do, I don't wanna see him hang.'

'Me neither, Pa,' remarked Brett.

'Wa'al, I can't exactly recall which of our circuit judges is due next,' said Grant.

Stone, for his part, remained silent. He reckoned that Abe Fletcher did deserve to end his short life on the gallows.

'Anyways, as a result of this attempt on our lives, I wanna see Abe one last time,' said the rancher.

'But why, Pa? What will that achieve?' enquired Brett.

'Yes. Surely meeting up with him again will only serve to distress you?' said Sally.

Robert B glanced at his daughter-in-law and smiled sadly.

'It's somethin' I've gotta do, my dear,' he replied.

'But. . . .'

He held up his hand.

'No buts,' he said. 'I'll explain when I return.'

'An' when will that be, Pa?' asked Brett.

'Some time tomorrow. I figure on ridin' with the marshal an' Mr Stone. When d'you expect to reach Calico City, gents?'

'Late afternoon, I guess,' said Grant.

'Then I reckon I'll do what you fellers are doin'. I'll rest up overnight an' then set out straight after break-fast. You can expect me late tomorrow afternoon. In

145

the meantime, I'll leave the ranch in your hands, Brett.'

Brett smiled. This would be the first time he had been left in sole charge. He would enjoy the challenge. Not that it would be too much of a challenge, he thought, for in Lew Todd he had an excellent foreman and most of the hands were pretty experienced.

'You can rely on me, Pa,' he said.

'I know I can,' said his father.

During the remainder of breakfast, the conversation turned to more mundane matters. Then, half an hour later, Brett and Sally Fletcher waved goodbye to the rancher, the marshal and the Kentuckian, as they rode off to join the trail that would lead them eastwards, past Snake Springs and on towards their destination, Calico City.

Marshal Dave Grant's guess proved correct. It was shortly after five o'clock when the three horsemen rode across the town limits and entered Calico City's Main Street. They trotted slowly down it and pulled up outside the Alhambra Hotel. Then, dismounting and hitching their horses to the rail outside, they entered and enquired of the reception clerk whether Abe Fletcher was in his room. The clerk replied in the affirmative and the trio trooped upstairs.

Abe Fletcher had spent an anxious time since Red Ned Davis and Hank Jolley departed to carry out their plan. He had paid a call to the Silver Dollar during the course of Friday morning in the hope that he might find Vic Morgan there. But, of course, he had not found him. He had questioned the proprietor, George Young, to be told that the homesteader had not so far visited the saloon that day. This seemed to Abe to make sense. He assumed that Morgan was proposing to remain quietly at home until the return of his cousin and Red Ned Davis.

Consequently, after consuming a couple of beers, Abe headed back across the street to the Alhambra Hotel. He rested in his room until noon, when he went and partook of some lunch at the hotel restaurant. As he left the restaurant, he glanced at the clock on the wall above the exit. Two o' clock. He smiled grimly. Six hours earlier, Vic Morgan's co-conspirators should have shot dead his father and his brother, making him the sole owner of the Triple F ranch. He prayed that nothing had gone wrong and made his way to the telegraph office. It was time to send that wire he had discussed with Vic Morgan.

Subsequent to sending off the wire, Abe had returned to his hotel room and stayed there, on tenterhooks, while he awaited a reply. He sat at the window overlooking Main Street, constantly on the look-out for the telegraphist, who he expected any minute to arrive with a response.

However, the minutes passed into hours and his anxiety increased. What if his brother's widow ignored his telegram? What should he do then? He felt the need to discuss this possibility with Vic

Morgan. Yet he dared not abandon his post, for fear that the anticipated response should arrive during his absence.

And so it was that, after a sleepless night, a highly agitated Abe Fletcher was again sitting at the window and staring out across Main Street when his father, the marshal and the Kentuckian hove into sight. He watched in disbelief as Robert Fletcher dismounted and, accompanied by the other two, marched into the hotel.

A few moments later, there was a loud knock on the door. Abe rose from his chair by the window and walked slowly, apprehensively, across the room. He pulled open the door just before Marshal Dave Grant could knock a second time. He stared at his father.

'Hi, Pa,' he mumbled.

Robert Fletcher regarded his son with an icy stare, stepped past the marshal and struck him a full-blooded punch on the jaw. Abe reeled backwards and collapsed on to the room's single bed.

Before he could rain any further blows down upon his first-born, Grant and Stone both grabbed hold of the rancher.

'Take it easy, Mr Fletcher,' growled Stone.

'Yeah. Beatin' the livin' daylights outta him ain't gonna help none. He's done for, anyways,' said Grant.

'That a son of mine should. . . .' began Robert B irately.

'I know. I know,' Grant interrupted him. 'You've

148

got every right to be angry, but Mr Stone's right. Your son's goin' down for a long, long time – assumin', of course, that he don't hang.'

'What . . . what are you sayin'?' gasped Abe.

His mind was in a whirl. The plot to eliminate his father had evidently failed. But how much did his father and the others actually know, and how much was mere conjecture? He determined to try to bluff his way out of the mess he found himself in, if he possibly could. As his father had survived the plot, Abe presumed that Brett had, too. Therefore, the Triple F was a lost cause. However, he still had the three thousand dollars his father had given him. Perhaps, he thought belatedly, he should have settled for that in the first place?

'I think you know exactly what I'm sayin',' said Grant.

Abe shook his head and attempted an air of injured innocence, but he didn't fool anybody.

'No, I swear I don't!' he cried. 'I was jest surprised to see Pa, that's all. An', when you struck me, Pa, wa'al. . . .'

'Shuddup an' listen to the Marshal! He's gonna read out a list of charges agin' you,' snarled Robert B.

Abe turned to face the peace officer.

'Go ahead,' he said, trying to exhibit a confidence he most certainly did not feel.

Marshal Dave Grant smiled thinly.

'Abe Fletcher, you are charged with conspirin' with others to murder your father, Robert B.

149

Fletcher, an' your younger brother, Brett Fletcher. Fortunately, the attempt upon their lives failed, but this does not lessen the enormity of your crime.'

'This is sheer nonsense!' declared Abe.' 'I ain't conspired with nobody.'

'No?'

'No, Marshal. You got proof of this?'

'Oh, yes, Mr Fletcher, I have proof! I got me witnesses.'

'Who, goddammit?'

'One: your fellow conspirator, Vic Morgan. An' two: Arizona Audrey, who overheard you plottin', an' who was tied up an' gagged an' kept prisoner in Vic Morgan's homestead. If'n' Mr Stone here hadn't come along an' rescued her, she'd be dead an' so would me an' Brett,' rasped Robert B.

'Aw, c'mon, Pa! You don't believe that! I wouldn't. . . .'

'Save your lies for the jury, Abe.'

'But, Pa. . . !'

'It's no use. Vic Morgan has confessed. I'll be holdin' you in a cell at the back of the law office till we can arrange for your trial,' said Grant.

Abe turned to his father.

'You can't let him do that!' he cried.

'I can, an' I will,' declared the rancher, and he went on to ask Grant, 'When is this trial likely to take place, Marshal?'

'Sometime towards the end of next week,' replied Grant. 'The circuit judge is due in town then to try a coupla fellers accused of cattle-rustlin'. I figure that once he's disposed of that case, he can try your son.'

'Last time you went to court, I pulled a few strings. But this time I won't be interferin'. When you killed poor ol' Willie Malone, I persuaded Judge Elmer Atkins, who owed me, to let you off with a custodial sentence. Otherwise, you'd have hanged for sure.'

'Yeah. An' I was grateful, Pa,' declared Abe fervently.

'Then you've a funny way of showin' it,' commented his father. 'Anyways, I won't be waitin' around for the trial. I got me a ranch to run. No doubt the marshal here will wire me an' let me know the outcome.'

'Sure will, Mr Fletcher,' said Grant.

'But, Pa, you can't jest abandon me!' protested Abe.

'You said the death of Willie Malone was an accident.'

'It was.'

'No, Abe, it wasn't. You deliberately heaved that poor ol' feller over that balustrade. Both me an' your ma knew you was lyin'. I took it hard, but your ma, she never got over the fact you'd committed murder an' lied about it. As sure as you killed Willie, you killed her. She died of a broken heart.'

'No, Pa!'

'Yes, Abe.' The rancher stepped up close to his son and, thrusting his hand deep inside Abe's coat, he pulled out the small canvas bag containing the three

151

thousand dollars he had given to him two days earlier. 'Don't reckon you'll be needin' this,' he remarked, stuffing it into one of his pockets.

'Hell, Pa, how'd you know it was still there, that I hadn't deposited it in the local bank?' demanded a surprised Abe Fletcher.

'A guess. But an educated one. I figured that, if it was your aim to kill me an' Brett an' then take over the ranch, you wouldn't be figurin' on stayin' around here. So, why bother to deposit the money in the bank?' Robert B turned and glanced at the peace officer and said, 'Take him away, Marshal. I don't wanna see him ever again.'

'No, don't s'pose you do.'

Grant produced a set of handcuffs and swiftly clamped them round Abe's wrists. Then, grabbing him roughly by the arm, the marshal marched him out of the room, down the stairs, out of the hotel and across the street towards the law office. Not that Abe went quietly. He protested all the way, pleading with his father to come to his rescue. But Robert B Fletcher shut his ears to the young man's cries.

Presently, when peace descended upon the Alhambra, the rancher turned to the Kentuckian.

'I could do with a stiff whiskey,' he said. 'Will you join me?'

'Sure will,' replied Stone.

The two men thereupon left the room and made their way to the Silver Dollar. The saloon was doing a roaring trade. There were three bartenders busy behind the bar, half a dozen sporting women in almost constant demand and the proprietor, George Young, presiding over the proceedings with a satisfied look on his face.

When Robert B Fletcher had bought two large whiskeys, he turned to Stone and raised his glass.

'Your good health!' he proposed.

'An' yours,' replied Stone.

They both took a good swig of the spirit.

'Ah, I needed that!' said Robert B. Then he pulled the small canvas bag out of his pocket and handed it to Stone. 'I'd like you to take this,' he said quietly.

Stone opened the bag and stared in astonishment at the wad of hundred dollar notes inside.

'I can't take this! I ain't no bounty hunter!' he exclaimed.

'It ain't bounty. It's simply a reward for savin' my life an' Brett's,' stated the rancher.

'But. . . .'

'No buts. I want you to have it, Mr Stone. If you hadn't stepped in an' forced a confession outa the homesteader, Vic Morgan, an' then recruited the marshal, me an' Brett would be dead men.'

'I can't take all the credit. It was Arizona Audrey who overheard the plot bein' discussed 'tween your son an' Vic Morgan. She could've sat back an' done nuthin'. But she didn't. She got involved an' darned near got herself killed in the process.'

'I guess so.'

'Therefore, I reckon she deserves to share in this

153

here reward.'

Robert B smiled and nodded his head.

'OK, Mr Stone, let's finish our drinks. Then we'll go meet this Arizona Audrey,' he said.

The two men quickly threw back the remainder of their whiskeys and left the saloon.

Upon their arrival a few minutes later at the bordello, they were greeted by Diamond Lil. They explained that they wished to see Arizona Audrey and were shown into the brothel-keeper's private sitting-room, where they found the erstwhile saloon singer.

'Jack, you're back!' she cried delightedly and threw herself into the Kentuckian's arms.

While they embraced and kissed, Diamond Lil excused herself and returned to the bordello's main room. There was a bar in one corner and those of her sporting women not currently engaged in their trade were either sitting, chatting and drinking with potential customers at the various tables scattered throughout the room, or simply conversing with one another at the bar. Diamond Lil slipped behind the counter and poured herself a glass of the white wine, which she had especially brought in from one of California's premier vineyards.

Meantime, Stone introduced Audrey to Robert Fletcher.

'Pleased to meet you, ma'am,' said the rancher, raising his Stetson. 'I wanna thank you for the part you played in savin' my life an' that of my son, Brett.'

'It was nuthin',' replied the blonde modestly.

'It weren't nuthin'. You put your life on the line,' stated Robert B.

'Even so, it was Jack who . . .' she began.

'It was both of us,' said Stone firmly. 'Therefore, it's only right that we should share the reward that Mr Fletcher has so generously given me.'

'What reward?' asked Audrey in surprise.

Stone produced the small canvas bag, which he had placed in the pocket of his buckskin jacket.

'This reward,' he said, taking the wad of one hundred dollar bills out of the bag.

'Holy cow!' exclaimed Audrey, as she realized the size of the reward. 'I can't take that!'

'That's what I said,' remarked Stone.

'You're both gonna take it,' retorted Robert Fletcher. 'An' while you're discussin' what you'll do with it, I'm gonna head back to the Alhambra an' book me a room for the night. Then I shall tend to my hoss. After that, I figure on gittin' somethin' to eat. Where do you suggest, Mr Stone?'

'The restaurant at the Alhambra serves a mighty fine meal,' said the Kentuckian.

'Fine. Gimme half an hour an' then join me there, the pair of you, for I ain't used to eatin' alone an' don't much relish the prospect. Therefore, I'd sure appreciate your company.'

'We'll be there,' said Stone.

'Yes, Mr Fletcher, we will be very happy to join you for supper,' added Audrey.

Left to their own devises, Stone and the blonde once again embraced and kissed. Indeed, it was some minutes before they parted and began to discuss what they should do with the money which the rancher had given them.

'So, what d'you plan doin' with your share, Jack?' enquired Audrey.

'Wa'al, I reckon I'll quit gunfightin',' he replied. 'I ain't gittin' no younger an' I'm weary of rovin' across the West. I intend that that shoot-out with them two outlaws on the trail outside Snake Springs should be my last. I'm hangin' up my gun an' headin' east to Kentucky, where I was raised. I'm from farmin' stock an' I shall use my share of the money to buy me some land an' raise stock an' grow crops.'

'You're gonna be a farmer?' cried Audrey.

'Yup. I wanna settle down an' sink some roots.'

The feelings and thoughts which he had experience two days earlier following their lovemaking in their room at the Alhambra Hotel, had strengthened. He wanted Audrey to settle down with him. The question was: did she feel the same?

'Wow! That sounds good,' she exclaimed.

'It does?'

'Yeah. I believe so.'

'An' what about you, Audrey? What are you aimin' to do with your share?'

'I . . . I'm not sure. I ain't had time to think yet.'

'I don't suppose you'd consider becomin' a farmer's wife?' he said quietly.

156

Their eyes met.

'Are you askin' me to marry you, Jack?' she murmured.

Stone smiled.

'I am,' he said.

'Oh, Jack!'

Audrey threw herself back into the Kentuckian's arms and a little time passed before either of them was able to speak. Then, eventually, the kissing ceased and they came up for air.

'So, whaddya say?' he said finally.

'Yes, Jack. 'Course I'll marry you,' she replied.

'First thing tomorrow mornin', we'll go see the local preacher an' git ourselves hitched,' declared Stone.

'An' then head for Kentucky?'

'Yup.'

'There's jest one thing I need to do first, an' I propose doin' it after we've had supper with Mr Fletcher. 'Deed, mine'll have to be a very light supper.'

'Why's that, Audrey? What're you proposin' to do?'

'You stated that you've had your final shoot-out. Wa'al, I reckon on makin' one last appearance on stage. I'm gonna persuade George Young to let me perform on his show tonight.'

'But he sacked you an' replaced you with a bunch of younger performers!'

'Even so. I shall make him an offer he won't refuse.'

'Oh! An' what's that?'

'I'm gonna offer to perform for free.'

'For free?'

'Yes. Why not? I reckon that, like you with your gunfightin', I have reached the point where I oughta quit. However, I would dearly like to hear an audience applaud me one last time. I want my swan song.'

'OK. Let's go have a word with Mr Young,' said Stone.

They left the bordello, bidding Diamond Lil farewell and telling her of Audrey's aim to perform that evening at the Silver Dollar. She, for her part, promised to come along and watch the show.

Their next port of call was the saloon, where Audrey put her proposition to the saloonkeeper. George Young quickly agreed for, although he felt that the blonde was past her prime and had consequently replaced her with half a dozen young dancers and singers known as The Sunshine Six, nevertheless he reckoned that the news that this was to be Arizona Audrey's last performance ever would surely bring in a pretty large crowd. Also, her offer to perform for free was something he could not refuse.

And so it was that, later that evening, The Sunshine Six performed a shorter song and dance show than usual and then, following their final curtain, George Young stepped on to the Silver Dollar's small stage and raised his arms.

'Ladies an' gentlemen,' he cried, although in fact the only 'ladies' present were his saloon girls, 'tonight the Silver Dollar proudly presents for your delectation the one and only Arizona Audrey, in what is to be positively her final performance prior to her retirement from the stage. Over the years she has wowed audiences across the length an' breadth of the West. An' so, without further ado, I give you . . , Arizona Audrey!'

George Young thereupon stepped to one side, the curtains re-opened and Arizona Audrey stepped forth on to the stage to thunderous applause. She was wearing her favourite gown, a full-length dress of bright scarlet, split up to the thigh and so decolette that her cleavage left very little to the imagination. He breasts remained small and firm like those of the six young dancers who had earlier graced the boards. Consequently, when she bowed at the end of each song, the applause and roars of delight were truly deafening.

She treated her audience to a rendering of five of the most popular songs of the day, all delivered in her usual slightly off-key warble. The fifth she announced would be her final number. And she finished by belting out 'See What the Boys in the Back Room Will Have'.

At the completion of this last song, the Silver Dollar's customers rose to their feet, whooping and hollering and applauding, guns were fired into the ceiling and glasses were raised in salute. At a table situated immediately in front of the stage were Diamond Lil, Marshal Dave Grant, Robert B

Fletcher and the Kentuckian, Jack Stone. And nobody was cheering louder or more vigorously than they were.

On stage, the small blonde songstress stood with tears of happiness trickling slowly down her cheeks, her mouth parted in a wide, delighted smile. It was truly a bitter-sweet moment. Tonight she was still Arizona Audrey. Tomorrow she would be Mrs Jack Stone.